Not Your Time

by Marjorie Malinowski

Copyright © 2010 by Marjorie Malinowski
First Edition — June 2013

ISBN
978-1-4602-1594-4 (Hardcover)
978-1-4602-1595-1 (Paperback)
978-1-4602-1596-8 (eBook)

All rights reserved.

No part of this publication may be reproduced in any form, or by any means, electronic or mechanical, including photocopying, recording, or any information browsing, storage, or retrieval system, without permission in writing from the publisher.

Produced by:

FriesenPress
Suite 300 – 852 Fort Street
Victoria, BC, Canada V8W 1H8

www.friesenpress.com

Distributed to the trade by The Ingram Book Company

dedicated to...

To my daughter Vanessa, who offered her continual support and encouragement as I moved forward to finish this first book.

To my daughter-in-law, Alisa, who read the draft and provided valuable insight along with her persistance to push me to move outside my comfort zone and continue to write.

Without these two beautiful, young women, my life would be very boring.

Chapter One

The room is small, and there are strange beeping noises. Ann tries to open her eyes, but everything is in a fog. There seems to be a bright light at the end of the bed. She can see her mother and father, standing there. Beside them, she sees two very good friends, the friends who gave her and her husband the two best gifts of a lifetime: their children. But they're all dead. Where is she, and what is happening?

It seems they are all talking directly to her. "You have to go back; it's not your time." In fact, each of them softly repeats this same statement. How can she go back when she does not know where she is?

"What do they mean it's not my time?" Slowly, the light dims, and she starts to feel pain again, as the wash of light disappears, along with her guests.

Where am I? She wonders. She thrashes about, trying to move her hands, but they appear to be tied down. She has something down her throat that is making her gag. She feels someone holding her hand. She again struggles to open her eyes. Ann looks into the beautiful blue eyes of Ed, her adoring husband of almost fifty years. Beyond Ed, she focuses on the doctor; it's her adopted daughter, Amy. Amy moves forward to check the machines that surround her mother. Just then, she hears a noise on her right side. She moves her head slightly and sees her adopted son, Jake.

"Glad you decided to wake up. You gave us quite a scare." Ed reaches over and kisses her forehead. Ann tries to smile, and it takes all her effort.

Ann gags as she struggles with the tube down her throat. "Don't fight that tube. Amy tells me they will remove it in just a few minutes. Have I told you today that I love you?" Ed holds her hand and calms her.

Amy moves forward, checks Ann's blood pressure, and listens to her heart. "Blood pressure has stabilized, and her heart is regular," she tells the nurse next to her. She leans forward and asks her mother if she needs something for the pain.

Ann realizes she hurts everywhere. Her chest is heavy, and shooting pain is pulsating through her heart. She can feel something that makes her look down. Her chest is covered in bandages, with tubes coming out the sides. She starts to panic, "What has happened to me?" It does not sound like her voice, but the words are loud enough for Amy.

Amy recognizes her mother's response. It is typical for someone who has suffered a heart attack and has to have emergency heart surgery.

"It's OK, Mom. You had a heart attack, and we had to do emergency coronary artery bypass graft surgery. We took a piece of vein from your leg and replaced the heart artery. We had to do this on three of your arteries. We got everything in time, and you're going to be fine. Lie back and try to relax. I'm going to give you something for the pain."

With that, Amy takes the needle from the nurse and inserts it into the tube attached to Ann's arm.

Ann relaxes and looks at her husband and her son. She's not sure how long she had been in this hospital bed, but both of her men had enough stubble to suggest they hadn't shaved for a couple of days. The dark shadows under their eyes make them both look haggard and exhausted.

"Mom, do not try to talk. Just give us a few minutes, and we will take the endotracheal tube out of your throat and set up a breathing tube that will allow you to speak. Maureen here will help, so just lie still for a couple minutes." Amy puts on a pair of rubber gloves.

Maureen takes the tray, puts on her rubber gloves, and gently removes the tube from Ann's throat. Ann gags and grimaces in pain, both from the tube moving up her raw throat and from the shooting pain from having to use her chest muscles.

Once the tube is out, Ann struggles with intense pain in her chest. She suddenly can feel the medication Amy has put into her IV tube and the pain is starting to slowly subside. .

Ann lies still, as Amy gently speaks to the nurse passing instructions to her. The new breathing apparatus is attached just inside Ann's nose, and she starts to feel the cool oxygen pass into her system.

"Mom, you need to remember to breathe through your nose and not your mouth." Amy watches as her mother starts to relax, and her breathing becomes soft and gentle.

"What happened to me?" Ann cannot remember anything after she went into the law office. Ann had worked at the law firm for many years, and though she had retired, she is required on occasion to stop in to witness wills and documents. It was good that she had not collapsed at home, where she would have been by herself.

"You were taken by ambulance to Riverside and then brought here." Ed stands beside her, holding her hand, as he had done for most of the time since she had come out of surgery and recovery.

"What time is it?" Ann asks.

"It's 2:30 in the morning," replies her son. "You were in surgery for several hours and several more hours in recovery. They just moved you into this room a short while ago. We have been so worried. Amy was in surgery with you the whole time." Jake smiles over at his little sister, Amy. She knows her stuff, and he's glad she was there when their mother was rushed in from Riverside. He's proud of what she has accomplished in just ten short years as a doctor.

The fact that both Amy and her brother, Jake, possess near-photographic memories helped them as children and on into their adulthood. Ann had been lucky that her sister Katherine's oldest son also has a similar memory retention ability. Having the knowledge and understanding of the problems related to children easily bored saved a lot of stress and Ann used many of the same activities passed on to her by Katherine. The kids kept busy with activities and challenges to keep them motivated. Both graduated from high school early and moved straight into university.

Fortunately, the principal at Riverside High School was friends with the president of the University of Calgary and was able to pull a few strings to get both Jake and Amy into good programs. Jake was working on several engineering courses while he was finishing twelfth grade. He received his engineering degree first and then decided to pursue a law degree after that. Amy started practicing medicine on her brother during hockey seasons; Jake was always suffering from something. Shoulder dislocations and knee injuries were commonplace because of the body checking allowed in pee-wee hockey in Alberta. Amy had always been fascinated with the workings of the heart and focused on medicine from an early age. After medical school, Amy took her residency with the University of Alberta. While there, she found herself sitting in on cardiac surgeries and met Dr. Morgan. He invited her back to Calgary to study under his team. It was his recommendation at his retirement that earned her the coveted spot of head of cardiology. Even after many years of retirement, Dr. Morgan is always there for her when she faces difficult tasks. He has agreed to help handle her mother's case for her.

Amy is the youngest doctor to be head of the cardiology unit at Rock Valley General Hospital in Calgary. It was her determination and hard work that earned her the respect of her peers and support of the board of directors at the hospital. Amy had been concerned about treating her mother, since the hospital frowns on doctors practicing medicine on family members. Amy did not want any special favors or put the staff in a difficult situation so she had her assistant go immediately to the hospital administrator/board CEO for permission and backup from the board to complete the surgery. She is fortunate to have such a strong relationship with her CEO and has been granted permission to do the surgery. Amy had to wait in the OR to get approval to save her mother's life. It was only when Ann's heart stopped a second time that the CEO gave immediate permission for the surgery. Amy is careful to make sure another doctor confirms all the treatments and is glad for the support of Dr. Morgan as the senior adviser on her mother's case.

The pain medicine is working, and Ann starts to feel more comfortable. Her motherly instincts take control. "You boys look terrible; why don't you go home and get some sleep. It's not my time today, and I have lots of people to watch over me," she said as yet another nurse drops in to check the machines.

With that, Ed and Jake plant a kiss on each of her cheeks and leave. Amy looks down at her mother. Ann sees the dark shadows under Amy's eyes; Ann knows the dark circles are from lack of sleep. She used to see them when the children came home on semester break after exams. "I'm going to follow your advice as well. They will call me if you need anything, but you should sleep for four or five hours at least. By then, I will be back. I love you Mom."

Amy speaks to the nurse in the room, who is typing something into the chart. She kisses her mother's forehead and leaves the room.

These drugs are great, Ann thinks. *No wonder people steal to get them.* Ann closes her eyes and drifts back in time.

As she drifts off, she feels herself in a time before she's Nana and Ed's Papa. She remembers the day Ed proposed to her, the day they got married, the day Ed got his job at the gas plant in Crossville, the day they bought their house, saying good-bye to her parents when they moved to Riverside for Ed's job, and her first day at the law office in Riverside. Those were the happy days. Then, she feels tears falling down her cheeks as she remembers the pain of her first miscarriage and then her second, third, fourth, and fifth, and the day Dr. Hammon told her no more tries. She would have to be satisfied being an aunt to her nieces and nephews and focus on a life with just her and Ed. She feels herself moving forward to the date of the tornado.

Chapter Two

There was Ed, standing by the garage door. She was living her life again; it was early morning on Friday, July 31.

"Don't forget, I need your car when you get back so I can do an oil change later today," Ed reminds Ann as she starts to back her Crown Victoria out of the garage.

"Don't worry. As soon as I pick up Jake so Jeff and Mary can go to her doctor's appointment, I will come right back. By the time your back from your meeting at the plant, I'll be here. Jake and I will have lunch ready. You promised him you would take him to the swimming pool, and you know he never forgets," Ann said as she backed up.

"I remember," laughed Ed. "Drive careful. I love you." He plants a swift kiss on Ann. It misses her lips but hits the side of her cheek as she starts to accelerate out of the garage.

Good thing she drives such a boat, Ed thought. Her desire to be early, especially when she usually runs late, always concerned Ed. He's the cautious driver, priding himself on never having an accident. Not that Ann's had an accident, but he worried just the same.

Ed hopped in his pickup and headed off to the gas plant for the regular Friday morning meeting. He enjoyed his job, but he hated the meetings. He would be glad when he would be ready to retire. He'd been with the same plant now for over twenty years. The plant didn't hold the same excitement, and he was tired of the politics the new company had brought. Big Sky Oil was a small, family-owned business, making good money. But when the old man died, the board of directors seemed lost as to who had the expertise to operate the small oil and gas company. With their former CEO, Edward Norway, now head of Pegasus, one of the largest oil and gas companies in Canada, it made sense to reach out and make a deal.

In a way, it was good that Pegasus bought the company, but there were so many changes and so much more paperwork, Ed began to lose interest in his job. He couldn't retire yet; he was too young, and besides, he promised Ann he would have a plan to keep himself busy. So far, he couldn't think of anything he wanted to do to keep himself occupied day in and day out.

Ed's plan was to work at the plant until he turned sixty-two and then spend the rest of his life trying to convince Ann that fishing and camping were fun retirement activities. Ann knew she would never like those outdoor activities, but she loved Ed and would do anything for him. Since they'd never have children, she knew she'd have to learn to like the camping and fishing.

It might have been different if they'd had kids, but Ann had tried to have a child so many times. Each time, she had more stress as she tried to carry a child to term, and it just made it worse. Ann kept trying until finally, Dr. Hammon had no choice: Ann had to have a hysterectomy. They'd married so young and still had lots of good life left in them, but with no children, the prospect of working hard for a future no longer held the same attraction.

They discussed adoption many times, but by the time they finally decided to start the paperwork, they were both older and no agency wanted to handle their file. They tried private adoption, and that was equally traumatic and unsuccessful.

It seemed God's plan was for them to have no children. Ann kept wondering why God was punishing her, but Ed kept reminding her they were part of a bigger, still unknown picture. It didn't keep Ed from having his moments of mourning for a child they would never have. Ed knew that Ann had thought about leaving him so he could find a woman who could give him lots of kids, but their love was so strong and deep. They somehow overcame the pain of so many miscarriages. Ed shuddered to think what life would be like without the love of his life. They were soul mates, and he knew it didn't matter if he had children. He showered Ann with his love, and together they had a good and full life.

When God brought Mary and Jeff Green into their lives; Ann and Ed felt this was God's answer to their prayers so they wouldn't feel so alone in life. They had adopted this young family from Newfoundland as their own when Mary and Jeff first moved to the area. It was fun to watch how their lives changed with the addition of their first son, Jake. Now, three years later, with another child on the way, Jeff and Mary would be happy for more help.

Ed and Ann had a chance to live their dreams through these two young people. It was sad to think they would be the only grandparent-type people these two babies would have in their lives. Both Jeff and Mary were only children, and both sets of parents had died shortly after Mary and Jeff had married. Mary's parents, Mary-Amy and Henry, owned their own convenience store and were in a terrible car accident on their way home one evening.

Jeff's parents, Jacob and Elizabeth, were both professionals: Jacob was a lawyer, and Elizabeth had been a bank manager. They both died of cancer within a year of each other. It had been hard on Jeff and Mary to lose both sets of parents within such a short time. With no attachments left in Newfoundland, Jeff and Mary moved out west, hoping for a new dream and to heal their wounds. Jeff found work on the rigs, and Mary discovered she was pregnant. They decided the quiet little rural town of Riverside fit their needs. They found a lovely acreage just outside of town and began to set down their roots for a new life together.

The little church community welcomed them, and Jeff felt secure that Mary would be looked after while he was away on the rigs. They quickly bonded with Ann and Ed. When the baby came early, Jeff was away, so Ann stepped into his shoes to be there with Mary until he made it home. Participating in the birth of Jake brought Mary and Ann even closer. Ann became Mary's adopted mother, always there when the baby was sick or teething or when Mary needed a shoulder on which to lean.

Jake was a colicky baby, and Ed was the only one who could put him to sleep for the night. This brought Ed and Mary together, and it was not long before Ed was providing all sorts of fatherly advice to both of the young couple.

Chapter Three

Ed looked at the skies in the south and west, and the clouds were beginning to look very ominous. It was strange to see how the clouds seemed to be coming from two distinct directions. He hoped Ann would pick up Jake and head straight back into town before the hail in those clouds hit. He just bought her that new car, and the last thing it needed was hail damage.

Ed turned on the news channel and started listening to the stock market as he headed east to the plant. He needed to be back by noon. He promised Jake they would go to the pool, and Jake loved the waterslide. It was hard on Ed's knees, but he needed the exercise and loved to watch Jake as they slid down the tunnel into the pool. It was worth the pain to hear his squeals of sheer joy and happiness.

Children were truly God's gift, and it was hard not to be angry about having so much love to share and no children of their own. But God had a plan, Ed kept telling himself. Ed somehow just knew His plan involved Jeff and Mary.

Ann looked at the clock; she had to hurry. Jeff and Mary had Mary's regular doctor appointment in Calgary, and Jeff had been concerned about the road construction on a new section of Deerfoot Trail, just inside the city limits.

Ann never knew where the time went. She was so sure she would be early and able to help get Jake ready to spend the day with her. She had taken the day off to spend doing all the fun things she imagined mothers do with their children.

Ann looked to the south. The clouds were churning like she hadn't seen in a long time. It almost looked like the tornado clouds she used to see as a young teenager in southern Saskatchewan. Her father made sure they never actually saw a tornado; she and her sister, Katherine, would be herded down into the root cellar along with her mom. When they usually came out, the garden would be in shreds from the hail. But, she was pretty sure that Alberta didn't have tornadoes. She had never heard any news reports about tornadoes, like they did when they lived in Saskatchewan. It must be a rain and hail storm. She had better hurry. She knew Ed wouldn't be happy if her new car was not in the shelter of the garage when the hail hit. Her last car carried the remnants of a hailstorm for two years before she hit a deer and the body shop pounded out all the little dents in the roof and trunk.

The acreage was just ahead. Jeff would already have the car loaded up, because he was always ahead of schedule. This habit must be from having to work so far away from home.

Ed always worked at the plant, at least for as long as they had been married, and even though he worked twelve-hour shift work, he was always home. Ann had never thought about how lucky she was not to be faced with the loneliness. She was happy to keep Mary and Jake company whille Jeff was away. They spent a lot of time together and had formed a strong bond.

Ann thought about her own parents, who were both gone as well. They both died of cancer within days of their sixth-ninth birthdays, three years apart. She had come to dislike July since both died in July, her dad on July 9 and her mother on July 15.

Suddenly, the wind seemed to lift her car. Her mind came back to the task at hand. She looked up and saw a huge tornado ahead of her. It was like watching the US documentaries and news about tornadoes and tornado chasers. This huge, rotating, funnel-shaped cloud reached from the ground high into the sky. It must have been several hundred feet up. It was moving so fast. At first, it seemed to be coming straight at her, but it suddenly changed direction. Though the tornado was moving away from her, the winds and blowing dirt were making it hard to focus and driving almost impossible. She could feel something hit her car, but dents were not her concern right now. Trying to keep the car on the ground was her whole focus.

How fast could this thing be moving? she thought.

She pounded her foot on the brake. Ann stopped right in the middle of the road and watched in horror as this massive tornado moved promptly to her left and seemed to be heading straight for the Green's acreage.

"*Oh God, what is happening? Please keep them safe.*" Ann didn't realize she was screaming, it was so loud and noisy. It sounded like she was right beside a huge freight train. She had her eyes fixed on events unfolding in front of her, as the huge tornado seemed to be moving faster and stirring up more dust and dirt. Then, the rain and hail started to beat down. Huge chunks of ice and dirt and rocks started pounding on the ground. They hit the ground so hard, mud splashed back up. Everything in its path seemed to be getting pulverized. They were pounding the car so hard; Ann thought the windows would break.

Without thinking about her own safety, Ann started to follow the tornado down the road toward the acreage. She had to warn Jeff and Mary. She turned the bend, and with horror, she saw her world churn in slow motion. The wind and rain were so bad she couldn't keep the windshield clean. Mud and water piled on top of her windshield. Hail pounded her car with huge chunks of ice. Tree branches were flying everywhere, but she could barely see what was happening through her muddy windows.

She lost her sense of direction. She knew she should to be at the acreage, but there was nothing: no house, no garage, no vehicles. *Where was she? Where were her friends?*

She stopped the car. She was sure she saw something. She opened the car door and held it, as the winds threatened to tear the door off the frame. Finnegan, the Green's Dalmatian, came running to her. He had blood all over him, but he kept coming. The hail was pounding on him, and the rain was almost as hard. She grabbed her coat from the seat next to her and ran toward him. She fell to the ground in front of the Dalmatian, and he ran straight into her arms. She held him and tried to cuddle him. The dog licked her face but whined with such pain and urgency. He was struggling to get out of her arms. He started to run, and Ann knew she had to follow him. Ann ran as fast as she could to keep up with him. She had no idea where she was going, but she knew Finnegan did, so she followed. The hail and rain hurt her as it pounded down, but she didn't have time to think about herself. She forgot about the tornado; she forgot about everything else but trying to keep up with the dog. She prayed as she ran.

Chapter Four

Ed was headed for the gas plant, thinking about the rest of his day.

Suddenly, something the radio announcer said grabbed his attention: tornado seen, no, tornado touched down, south of town. What town did he hear? Was the tornado south of Riverside or Huntersville, which town? He changed to the local radio station.

The radio station was full of static now, and he couldn't hear anything. Must be Huntersville, since the station was located on the south side of the town, and that would explain the static. Something told him to turn around and go back to Riverside. Without thinking, he found himself slowing down, turning around in the middle of the road, and heading back to town.

At that moment, he saw the tornado; it was definitely on the ground somewhere close to Riverside. It was massive, since he could see it and it was still a distance away. He pressed his foot hard on the gas to get to town as quickly as possible.

Ed was a part-time firefighter in town, and everyone would be needed if this thing hit the town. They had talked about training for such a disaster, but Alberta never has tornadoes, so it was a low priority for the men. He stopped the truck and dug out the bag phone he had as a member of the fire department. He had never used it but hoped someone was on the system at the town office to hear him. Sure enough, Mike Connors, the town foreman, was there and answered.

"Mike, sound the alarm. This thing is unbelievable. I have never seen a tornado, but this looks worse than anything I've ever saw on TV." Ed didn't realize he was shouting.

"Already done. We are heading to the station now."

"Do you know where it has set down?"

"Nope, but it's not within the town limits, I'm calling the RCMP now. I will call you back."

"Ann's headed for the Green's to pick up Jake. Can you confirm it's not in that direction?"

"Hold on." Mike's other phone, the station communication telephone, was ringing. Mike spoke into the second phone, but held the phone close so Ed could hear the conversation.

"South of town about one mile. Emergency vehicles are getting organized to move out."

Ed's heart sank. He started to pray for Ann and the kids. He sped up his truck. He had to get there, Ann needed him, and he couldn't let her down.

Chapter Five

Ann hurt everywhere, with more pain coming every time another hailstone hit her. They were the size of golf balls. She had no idea they could hurt so much. Finnegan was stumbling in pain, but he wouldn't stop. She kept following him. It seemed like forever, but she was sure it was just a matter of seconds, although time seemed to be standing still.

She knew she had to be in the yard. They were following the road, but as she struggled to see through the rain and hail, she couldn't see the house or the garage. She headed for the old barn, since that was where Finnegan was running. He ran past the barn, falling down several times. Each time he fell down, Ann was able to get closer. In front of her stood the old willow tree, on which Finnegan seemed to have focused. It was decades old and had always been a source of pride to Mary and Jeff. Ann thought she saw something: sure enough, Jake, in his little red coat, was sitting there. She quickly reached him and scooped him into her arms and turned, as Finnegan guided them back to the barn.

Inside the barn, Finnegan fell again. This time, he didn't get back up but lay there, whimpering in pain. She had to make sure Jake was OK before checking on Finnegan. Jake looked up into her face and gave her a big grin. "Why are you so wet, Nana? My raincoat kept me dry." Ann, with tears running down her cheeks, just gave him a big hug.

The strangest thing was that Jake was bone dry. There wasn't a bruise or sign of any hailstone damage on his face, arms, or body. It was as if a huge set of arms had been wrapped around him, keeping him safe. "Granddad Jacob kept me dry," he said.

Ann didn't pay much attention to his babbling. He was safe, and that was what mattered. Ann looked around and found an old blanket sitting on the tractor. She put Jake on the seat of the tractor and told him not to get down.

He was happy and started "driving" the tractor, as he did often when his father was busy working in the garage.

Ann bent down and checked out Finnegan. He had several nasty wounds that had blood oozing out of them, but from what she could tell, he was breathing strong, so Ann wrapped him in the blanket she had found to keep him warm in case he went into shock.

She checked her arms and legs. She had several nasty cuts and, judging by the welts on her arms and legs would be bruised by morning. She felt her head. There had been some hard hits, and there were tender spots, but otherwise she was fine.

Ann ventured to the door of the barn. The hail and rain were slowing down, and she could see the yard. She could see the basement of the house and the pad where the garage used to sit. But where was the house, and more important, where were Jeff and Mary? She knew neither of them would have left Jake alone, but she couldn't see them anywhere.

"Please God, let them have found shelter and be safe." Ann prayed those few words over and over again.

Suddenly, she saw flashing lights. She stepped out of the barn and waved her arms. Great, it was Mike, a friend from the church, at the wheel of the emergency vehicle. He drove straight up to the barn and jumped out to give Ann a big hug. "Are you OK?"

"Yes," she replied. "Except for a few scrapes and bruises, I'm fine."

"Where is everybody else? Have you seen or heard anything?" Mike took control of the situation, asking questions and talking into his portable radio.

"I have Jake here in the barn; he's on the tractor. Finnegan is really hurt badly, but I didn't want to leave Jake alone to go any further. I don't know where Jeff and Mary are. I just know they would never leave Jake alone, and I just feel in my heart that they're in trouble."

Mike called his men to start looking. They spanned out and began a search of the property. Ed suddenly appeared from nowhere. It was still raining, but the hail and wind had started to subdue.

He shouted at Ann, "Are you OK? Where is Jake? Where are Jeff and Mary?" He gathered Ann into his arms and held her so tightly Ann thought he would break her ribs. "Thank God you're OK."

Jake tugged at his pant leg. "Papa, can I have a hug, too?" he asked.

In one quick movement, Ed swooped down and picked up Jake, while continuing to keep his arm around Ann. "I always have hugs for you, little buddy," he said.

"Hey Ed, can you come and give us a hand here?" Mike had a strange look on his face. Ann had never seen such an expression. A chill ran down her spine, and she took Jake out of Ed's arms.

Ed turned to Ann before he followed Mike. "You stay here with Jake, since we're not sure what we have here. He's had enough trauma for one day."

Ed and Mike walked out into a dip in the field. Ed could see blue fabric, and it was covered in blood. Then he saw the strawberry hair, and he started to run; it was Jeff. But where was Mary? Then he saw a hand around Jeff's waist.

Ed reached Jeff first. He could see blood and cuts everywhere on his body. He reached down to touch him. His hand touched a cold neck, cold like he had never before felt. He knew instantly Jeff was dead. He reached for Mary's hand, expecting the same, but her hand squeezed back. "Mike, bring the truck and fast. She's still alive."

Carefully, he moved Jeff away and saw Mary folded under him, her body twisted in such a way that suggested several badly broken bones. He bent down to Mary, and she started to cry. "Ed, please save our baby," she pleaded.

Mike was back in a flash with the ambulance. He had the stretcher and Stan, one of the local EMTs. Quickly, Stan checked her pulse. He gave a pained look back at Ed and Mike. Together, they lifted Mary onto the stretcher. She saw Jeff and shouted at them, "Take Jeff first. He's hurt worse than me. He took the force of the wind and kept me safe. You have to save him first."

With that, Mary passed out. Stan quickly pulled up the covers and used the radio to have the hospital call Stars Air Ambulance, since he already knew they couldn't handle the kind of massive trauma Mary had sustained. Plus, he knew she would need immediate surgery if they were going to save the baby.

Ed went over to Jeff and put a blanket around him. He looked back at Mary, just in case she was watching. Ed bent down to appear to be attending to Jeff. This was completely for Mary's benefit, as Jeff was already in a better place.

Suddenly, out of nowhere, there was Dr. Hammond. Stan turned, "Mo, thank God you're here. She's in big trouble." Dr. Hammond moved in to take control. Shouting medical terms to Stan, they both worked on Mary. Within a few minutes, the STARS helicopter landed, and Mary was moved inside.

Ed moved back to keep out of the way of the giant blades. Dr. Hammond and the STARS attendant had moved at lightning speed, loading her up and took right back off.

"You can meet us at the Rock Valley," Dr. Hammond shouted back at Ed.

Dr. Hammond had been shouting orders into his phone. "Have the trauma unit on standby and the surgery room ready to go. We also need a paediatric trauma specialist on site. Call my office to get her blood type and get blood there; we are going to need lots."

With that, Ed couldn't hear anymore, as the STARS helicopter took off.

Ed walked back to the barn. There was nothing else he could do in the field. A second ambulance was putting Jeff on a stretcher to take to the hospital; he would be declared dead on arrival. He looked up and saw Ann. Her eyes said it all: tears were flowing uncontrollably down her face as she clung to Jake. Ed gathered both of them into his arms and prayed for Mary and the doctors.

"Can we go for a ride on the big 'copter like Mommy?" Jake was unaware of the trauma unfolding around him. Ann and Ed turned their focus on this little boy, who had no doubt seen more today than any child should have to witness and experience. But, he seemed to have taken his ordeal in typical Jake stride.

"Let's get the big truck and take Finnegan to the vet, OK?" Jake looked at Finnegan.

"I want down," he told Ed.

Ed let him down, and Jake ran over to Finnegan and planted a big kiss on the dog's lips. "You're going to be just fine; it's a long way from your heart." Jake repeated the words his father always told him whenever he got a scratch. He had no idea what it meant or how badly hurt his best friend was. Ed and Ann looked at each other. They realized that Jake was like a little parrot with one incredible memory. Both of them prayed that Finnegan would be OK. He was such a good dog, and he was Jake's best friend.

Ed walked back to the car. It had a car seat, so Ann could bring Jake to town. A horn honked. It was Mike again, and he had brought Ed his truck. "I figured you'd want to take the dog to the vet in the truck," he said as he got out. Together, they lifted Finnegan into the truck; the blanket was wrapped around him. "I called ahead. Dr. Dave is waiting for you now."

"Thanks Mike, are you waiting for the RCMP to come and finish up?"

"Yes, but it may be a while. They're sending a team from the city. Every man and car between here and Edmonton is busy. Seems this beast set down in several locations before it hit the capital big time, lots of dead and injured unbelievable damage."

With that, Ed left for the vet clinic. He drove to where Ann and Jake waited. "I will meet you back at the house. You might want to quickly wash up and change. I will pick you and Jake up to head into the Rock Valley. I'll call from the clinic and let you know how long you have before I come."

As Ann followed Ed, her eyes wandered back to Jake. He seemed oblivious to what had just happened. Her eyes went back to the road. She started to look around, taking in the damage around her. Trees uprooted, power lines broken like toothpicks, lumber and garbage everywhere. Ann and Jake got into the car, and as she turned onto the main road, she saw Ed pull over. There in the ditch and field were pieces of the Green house.

It was incredible; she saw that Jake had already fallen asleep, so Ann stopped. Together, she and Ed walked into the ditch. Pictures, broken furniture, and pieces of clothing were everywhere. Ann bent down and started to pick up a couple of family pictures. *This could be all that Mary has left,* she thought. She found a photo album of their wedding pictures and a couple of pictures of Jake that had been hanging in the hallway. Ann gathered up the first armful. Ed had already put a pile of belongings into the trunk of her car. They were wet and muddy.

"Ed, you need to get Finnegan to the vet. I will gather up a few more things and then head to the house."

"No you will not," said a voice behind her.

It was their neighbor and friend, Bert Jones. He worked with Ed at the plant. Bert had been monitoring the emergency radio at the plant and got everyone mobilized to help. "I brought everyone from the meeting. We'll load up the trucks with everything we can and bring it all back to your house. You two look after Mary and Jake. We can handle this stuff." Once they finished there, they would see if anyone else in the local area needed them.

Chapter Six

Ed drove straight to the vet. Dr. Dave and his staff stood waiting. They knew they would probably have several more animals before the day was finished. Mike had telephoned to let them know Ed was bringing Finnegan, the Green family pet. He had also told them the situation with Jeff and Mary.

This is how it is in a small town. Everybody knows everything, and whether it is good news or bad, it spreads like wildfire. Today was no exception.

As he drove up to the clinic, Ed said to Finnegan, "You hang in there, buddy. Jake is really going to need a friend now, more than ever."

Then he said another prayer, asking for another favour, "Lord, keep this dog safe, and bring him back healthy for Jake. This little boy is going to need all the love we can give."

Dr. Dave grabbed the door of the truck and gently lifted Finnegan out. He whispered into Finnegan's ear, telling him he was going to be fine. He knew Finnegan hated going to his clinic, as did almost every dog did after the first trip and set of needles. Finnegan licked his hand, as if he knew that Dave would do everything he could to take away the pain and fix his wounds.

Ed was getting out of the truck, but Dave looked up as he carried the dog inside. "You have more important things to do. Make sure Jake is OK and then you need to head to the hospital. You and Ann are the closest to family Mary has, and you need to be there for her."

Dr. Dave went inside, and his assistant, Jennifer, called back to Ed, "I will call you as soon as Finnegan is checked out. We should be calling by the time you're cleaned up and ready to head to the hospital."

Ed didn't need to be reminded twice of what else had to be done yet today. When he arrived home, he didn't bother to drive into the garage, since Bert had several company trucks lined up to unload in the garage. "What a mess. Everything is wet and muddy."

"Don't worry," said Bert. "I have called Bruce and Connie, along with Joyce and Al, and they have arranged for a team to come here and sort things out. By the time you get back from the hospital, everything should be cleaned and organized." Bert was a great friend. He had taken charge here, just like he did at the plant when things needed to be done and done properly. There was never a halfway when Bert was involved.

Ed took off his shoes at the door and looked down at his socks. Then he took off his socks and went to find the garden hose. He was covered in mud. His truck must be a mess. He hosed himself off the best he could. He went back to the deck, stripped off his pants and shirt by the door, and put the wet mess in a pile.

He went straight to the shower. Ann was in the spare room they had organized for Jake when he slept over. Ann and Jake were discussing the importance of wearing underwear. Ed smiled and closed the bathroom door. The warm water felt good on his cold, wet skin. He had no idea he was that cold and that wet.

His shower didn't last long, since the bathroom door opened and in marched Jake. He slid open the glass door of the shower and looked inside. Ed was not used to such a young audience. Ann was right behind Jake and picked him up, mentioning a quick sandwich while Ed was finishing the shower. She had set out dry clothes.

"Can you hurry so we can get to the hospital? Mo had one of the nurses call. Mary is in the trauma unit now."

"I'm out already," Ed hollered back. He didn't need a chance that his little buddy would come back in the room to watch him shower. He was dressed and ready in minutes.

Out in the garage, Bert and his team were sorting and cleaning the remaining property that belonged to Jeff and Mary. They had found toys, baby clothes, everything that could be salvaged.

"I have the car ready for you to head to the city." Bert handed Ed the keys. He took Jake from Ed and put him in his car seat.

"There you go, little fellow. Let's keep you safe and in one place while Ed drives." Bert talked to Jake as Ann and Ed got into their car.

"Call us when you have news. I have called the prayer line. Every church in town knows about Mary and Jeff. The Lord will be busy with all the prayer requests that He is receiving right now." Bert was one of the elders at the church, and he had handled this along with probably other details Ed and Ann would learn about later.

"The trip to the hospital is going to take time," said Ann.

"Let's ride in the 'copter, like Mommy did," Jake offered his suggestion.

"Sorry, Jake," said Ed, "we don't have a helicopter to get us there."

Just then, a police cruiser was in front of the car. Constable Ken Conway of the local RCMP detachment was ready. "Follow me," he said, "I can get you to the hospital faster with the lights."

Jake was so excited. "Look at the police car. I have one just like it; remember, Santa Claus brought it to me?" He pointed to Ken, "Let me out of the car seat so I can see."

"Sorry, little buddy, you have to stay buckled up, because we are going to be driving very fast." Ed buckled himself up, and away they went.

The trip to the Rock Valley was fast. Ed had trouble keeping up with Ken, as he had lights flashing and cars were moving out of the way. The news of the tornado was now on every station across Canada. People knew what had happened, and they were all moving out of the way of every emergency vehicle.

When they reached the hospital, Ken parked them in the area reserved for emergencies. Ken took Ed and Ann, along with Jake, through the emergency room doors. There was a nurse at the door to take them up to the family area, where the doctors would be able to explain what was happening. Ann knew things must not be good for Mary, and this special attention confirmed her worst thoughts.

Ann took a quick look around the room. She was surprised to see her boss, James Stewart, in the room. "What are you doing here?" she asked.

"I heard what happened and knew you were going to need these papers that give you consent to discuss Mary and her situation. Both Mary and Jeff appointed you and Ed executors of their wills. They also made enduring power of attorney documents and appointed both of you to act on their behalf if they were incapacitated and unable to make decisions for themselves. You will need this today. I wanted to make sure these documents were here for you." James handed Ed the documents and gave Ann a big hug.

James, turning to leave the room, stopped and looked back. "Don't worry about us at the office. Jean and I can handle it for as long as it takes. Jean sends her love and prayers as well. If you need anything else, and I mean anything, you call. Use my private cell; you have the number."

Just then, a doctor and nurse came into the room. The nurse, her name tag said Doreen, bent down in front of Jake and asked him if he like teddy bears. "I sure do," said Jake, and he took her hand to follow her out of the room.

"Hello, my name is John Frazer. I'm the head of the trauma unit here. We need to discuss Mary and her options. I understand from her lawyer that you have the authorization to make decisions."

He led Ed and Ann over to the chairs in the corner of the room, and they sat down. The room was brightly coloured, with doors opening onto a small courtyard. The grass was lush and green, with flowers filling pots and small patches. This garden reflected the love and care that someone gave it. It was a masterpiece of worship and devotion. The petunias spread out across the containers, and colour—bright purple and hot pink, with hints of white and yellow—splashed down the sides. If Ann were not so overwhelmed by concern for Mary, she would have gone out and sat on the small bench. Maybe tomorrow she would want to enjoy the love of nature that her Lord had so richly provided. Right now, she needed to focus on Mary and her unborn child.

She realized Dr. Frazer had started to talk. "I'm sorry," said Mary, "would you mind starting again?"

"As I was saying, Mary has sustained multiple fractures to her extremities; her arms and legs are broken in several places as well as several broken ribs. Both of her lungs have been punctured. She has internal injuries and internal bleeding. She's in critical condition." He realized he needed to allow both of these people time to absorb and understand. He started again.

"Mary is a strong woman, but besides her internal injuries, she has suffered massive head trauma. She's bleeding internally, and we need to try to stop the bleeding. The baby has a steady heartbeat, and at this point, could survive an early birth."

Ann and Ed held hands and nodded in response. They knew it was up to the Lord whether Mary and her little girl would survive. Was it her time? That was a question only God could answer.

Dr. Frazer continued, "She's in and out of consciousness. She wants to see you both alone before she sees Jake. I have given her pain medication, but she's still in a great deal of distress. Once you have seen her, I would like you to see the nurse and make sure all the necessary paperwork is completed. You can do that while I prepare for surgery. I have an excellent paediatrician ready to assist me. We'll try our best, but it will be up to her and God as to the outcome. We don't have much time."

With that, he left, and another nurse, Joan, came in and took them into the ICU room. Ann was not really prepared for what she saw. There were machines and nurses and doctors everywhere. Mary had blood and bruises on her face and arms. Her eyes were closed. She had an intravenous line in each arm. Her beautiful blond hair was caked with mud and blood. Ann went over and gently took her hand. Mary struggled to open her eyes. She tried to smile, but she moved slightly and grimaced in pain.

"Lie still Mary," said Ed. "We are right here for you. You're strong, and you will have to fight hard to win this battle."

"I know I don't have much time, but I want you both to promise you will make sure the doctors save my little girl. I want you to watch over Jake and Amy when I'm gone. You will be all they have, but I have faith that you'll love them as much as Jeff and I." Mary spoken softly, and Ed and Ann nodded.

Mary kept on. "Her name is Amy, after my mother, and Elizabeth, after Jeff's mom. Jeff and I chose her name just last night. Strange how things happen. One day she has no name, and the next day we know without a doubt that she's Amy Elizabeth. But now I need to speak to Jake. Can you bring him to me so I can say good-bye?"

Ann couldn't hold back her tears. She sobbed quietly as Mary spoke, "Ann, it's OK. I know what has to happen. Just keep your promises to me, and I'll love you both forever." Another nurse gently lifted Mary's head and pulled a surgery cap over her head.

Just then, Doreen brought Jake in the room. He was holding a teddy bear covered in Band-Aids. "Look, Mommy, teddy is all better. I fixed him up just like the doctor is gonna to fix you." Jake held out the teddy bear for all to admire his handiwork.

Doreen lifted him onto a chair beside Mary. "Hi, Mommy. You have mud on you. You need to have a bath."

Ann was amazed that Jake didn't seem to be frightened or upset at the sight of his mother in the ICU room, with all the machines and strange noises.

He reached out and grabbed Mary by the hand. Mary spoke to him, "Mommy has to go away, and Nana and Papa are going to keep you and your little sister. Is that OK with you?"

Jake held tightly onto the bear with one hand and onto his mother with the other. While he couldn't possibly understand the situation, he loved to spend time with Nana and Papa, so he smiled the big, lopsided grin he had inherited from his father.

"Oh boy. I can go swimming every day with Papa?" Even at the age of three, Jake knew how to bring a room to laughter.

"Well, maybe not today, but soon," his mother promised. "Give me a big kiss and a hug, and out you go with Papa."

Doreen gently lifted him, and he planted a big wet kiss on his mother's cheek and wrapped his arms around her neck. The nurse knew how much pain this must be causing this brave, young mother and admired her courage and strength.

Jake finally let go, and he saw a tear roll down his mother's face. "Are you going to cry like you do when Daddy goes to work?" Suddenly, he realized his father was not in the room. He looked around at all the nurses and doctors. "Hey where did Daddy go?"

Ed picked him up and looked at Ann and then at Mary. Mary tried to smile. "Tell him the truth. We never lie to him when he asks questions. Sometimes not all the truth, but as much as his little head and heart can handle. I have a date with doctor and then with my family. I love you all, and remember to tell Jake and Amy every day how much I love them both. Oh, and Jeff wants you to make sure you give 'em lots of hugs."

Mary closed her eyes. Doreen reached over and checked a monitor. She called Joan. "The baby's heartbeat is starting to fall. Let's get moving to ER now."

Ann hugged Mary one last time and left the room, tears flowing down her face uncontrollably. She saw a washroom across the hall and stepped inside to wash her face. Now was not the time to fall apart; she had to be strong.

Chapter Seven

Ann felt a little better after she washed away the tears. Her eyes were red, but she couldn't do anything about that. She also knew there would be many more tears shed yet today. As she entered the little waiting room, she noticed the pictures on the walls. They looked like the artwork of small children. The room was painted a bright yellow, and the sun was shining brightly into the room. The room felt warm.

Ed and Jake were sitting at a small table; Jake was showing Ed how to put even more Band-Aids on the poor little teddy bear. Jake didn't seem to pick up on the pain Ed showed as he looked toward Ann.

"We thought we lost you."

"Sorry, I took a few minutes in the washroom to try to freshen up a bit. It didn't help much, but I needed to brace myself for the rest of today." Ann walked over to the little red table and bright blue chairs. "Can I join you two fine gentlemen?"

Jake looked up at her and said, "Do ya know how to put a Band-Aid on an owie?"

"Well, I think so, but maybe you should show me, just in case I hurt myself."

For the next hour, Ed and Ann kept Jake busy, playing with puzzles and reading stories. Jake started to yawn. "Would you like to curl up in this big chair with me and close your eyes?" The warm sun on her was making her yawn as well.

"Can I have this big chair all by myself? I like how it feels on my toes." Jake had taken off his shoes and socks earlier.

"No problem. Would you like a cover?"

"Nope, not cold." Jake crawled up onto the chair. He lay back and closed his eyes. He was asleep within minutes. Ann covered him up with a small blanket she found on the back of the sofa.

Ann got up and went over to the little sofa, where Ed was sprawled out. His long legs reached out into the room. He sat up as Ann approached. "This is taking a long time. I wish someone would tell us what is happening."

"Would you like me to see if I can find a nurse?" Ann asked as she reached out a brushed Ed's thick auburn hair off his face.

"No, I'm hoping no news is good right now." Ed patted the sofa, and Ann sat down. He put his arm around her slim shoulders. "How do we tell this little boy about his dad next time he asks?"

"I guess we tell him the truth. He has gone to be with Jesus, and someday he will get to see him again."

Ann looked at the little side table and realized she had put down the envelope James Stewart had given her earlier. She picked it up and opened the little tab that held it shut. She took out the first set of documents. It was the "Last Will and Testament of Jeffrey Jacob Green." Ann knew these documents, since it was her job at the law office to handle estate paperwork, and wills were a big part of the workload. She quickly read it over, typical document, but she was surprised she hadn't prepared it. It was normally her job at work to handle preparation of wills and estate documents. She looked at the last page and saw that James and Jean Stewart had signed it. James must have prepared it himself. Edward Anthony Murray and Ann Marie Murray were appointed executors and guardians of his estate. Ann knew that Mary's Will would be a mirror of Jeff's will. She passed it over to Ed to read.

Ed didn't handle legal documents very often, so he sat back and started to read it carefully. He stopped several times to ask Ann about a paragraph and its meaning.

Ann checked the envelope again; an additional set of documents were paper clipped together. They were matching powers of attorney, authorizing Ed and Ann to make any decisions should either Jeff or Mary be unable to do so. They also both wanted to be organ donors. She knew these documents by heart as well.

She wondered when Jeff and Mary had James do up these documents. She checked the last page for a date. Wide-eyed, she turned to Ed. "Do you see? They did up these documents just two days ago. I wonder what made them get these things done without speaking with us about it."

"I guess you will have to ask James when you see him at the office, if you don't see him before," Ed muttered. He was still trying to concentrate on what he was reading.

"I have to speak to the nurse. Both Jeff and Mary are organ donors, and the hospital should be told." Ann left the room, coming back in about ten minutes.

"Any news?"

"No, nothing yet."

Ann leaned back on the soft, next to Ed, and closed her eyes. Her eyes were burning from the salt from her tears. She hurt from all the hail and knew she would be covered in bruises tomorrow. She was too tired to sleep and needed to have some quiet time to pray. She wondered why this was happening and what else was in God's plan for them. She worried about how she would explain all this to Jake. She kept praying, asking God to protect Mary and her baby and keep them here for Jake's sake, as well as her own. As she prayed to God, she felt a comfort and warmth cover her. She opened her eyes and saw Ed had slipped off the sofa and was on his knees in prayer. She quietly slipped down beside him, and he reached over and held her hand. Together, they prayed for the mother and child who were in a room not far away and for the little boy curled up and asleep in the chair next to them.

Chapter Eight

Ann felt lips brush past her cheek and arms move onto her shoulders. She turned, expecting to see Ed, but realized he was still holding her hand as he continued to kneel in prayer. Her sudden movement caught Ed by surprise, and he released her hand. "Are you OK?" he asked.

"Strange, I thought you had leaned over to kiss my cheek. But, you're on the wrong side, and I felt arms around me." Ann rose and turned around.

It was late already, and the yard lights in the little garden started to turn on. She noticed Jake was up. He stood next to the garden doors and appeared to be in a deep conversation with someone. She quietly moved forward to see what he was up to.

Jake stood tall, with both arms outstretched. She heard him talking. "But Mommy, I want to go with you and Daddy. Why do I have to stay here with Nana and Papa?"

Ann couldn't believe her eyes or her ears. To whom was he talking? It looked like someone was holding his hands. She didn't say a word and motioned for Ed to be quiet and to come closer to her.

Jake continued his one-sided conversation. "Yes, Daddy, I will look after my little sister. I will be a good boy. But why can't I come with you? I don't want to stay here by myself, I want to go with you." He started to cry softly. "I'm a big boy, but I want to go with you."

Tears ran down his face, and Ann felt tears running down her cheeks. Ed put his arms around her and gave her a quick hug before he moved forward and gathered Jake up into his arms.

"I think you need a bear hug," he said to Jake as he lifted him up into the air.

"Mommy and Daddy want me to stay with you and Nana, but I want to go with them." Jake continued to sob.

"It's OK. I want your mommy and daddy to stay, too, but Jesus wants them to come see Him for a while, so you and your new sister can come stay with us until you're ready to see your mommy and daddy again."

Tears were forming in Ed's eyes as he spoke, because he knew what had just happened. In Sunday school a few weeks earlier, they had studied the perceptive powers children have, and he believed children saw angels and deceased people because of their innocence and love for all things.

Ed had read that children are fresh from God and still have the eyesight to see the miraculous with ease. As a child, they share from their hearts and believe what they see. There have been many stories about angel encounters. He also knew that God would have wanted Mary and Jeff to be able to say good-bye to their beloved little boy one last time.

Ed turned to Ann; he knew what would happen next. He understood the conversation Jake had just had, and he believed both Mary and Jeff had passed over into the light and were in Heaven.

Just then, Dr. Frazer, still wearing his surgical scrubs, came into the waiting room. He took off his cap and held it in his hand. This was the hardest part of being a doctor: sometimes you didn't save your patient, and it was always up to the doctor to bring this sad news to the family members.

Ed, still holding Jake, came over and took Dr. Frazer's hand. "It's OK, we already know. Mary has left us."

"Well, yes, but technically no; her organs are being kept alive on life support. We'll start to remove them. They will go to several hospitals, and there will be several prayers answered today. You will not be alone. She may not be with us, but she has left you a beautiful little baby girl. She's fine. The nurses are just cleaning her up. If you wait a few minutes, someone will be in to take you to your new little daughter. I wish I could have saved them both, but Mary had so many injuries. We did everything we could."

"We know you did," said Ann, and she moved forward and gave the doctor a hug. "Jake just said good-bye to his mom and dad, and we're all ready to see this new little baby, aren't we Jake?"

"Can I hold the baby?" Jake wiggled to be let down, and Ed bent down and put him on the floor. "Her name is Amy, you know. My mommy told me that."

"Yes, her name is Amy. Amy Elizabeth Green Murray. That's what her name is, just like your name is Jacob Jeffrey Green Murray." Ann figured he might as well start getting used to adding Murray to his name. He was so young; it wouldn't be hard to make the change.

Nurse Doreen came in. "Are you all ready to see the new baby? Come with me. You need to wash your hands when you hold a baby, you know, Jake." She took Jake's hand and off they went.

"God does answer prayers. You just never know when or how His plan works, but knowing He has a plan will be your comfort. If you need anything, just ask." Dr. Frazer held open the door. He knew Ann and Ed had just undergone a life-changing experience—in fact, several life changing experiences—in the past twenty-four hours.

Ann and Ed left the little waiting room and walked through the doors into their new life as parents.

Chapter Nine

Ann suddenly feels she's not alone; she stirs and realizes she's back in the hospital. Her memories of earlier in the evening return to her. She's had heart surgery. Everything is OK. A nurse is checking the dressings on her chest. She looks down and gasps. She has a wide, long, and very ugly gash from the top of her chest as far as she could see without raising her head off the pillow. The gasp alerts the nurse that Ann is awake and conscious.

"It's OK, dear. I'm just checking to see how the surgery went. Everything looks just fine. You lay back and rest. I'll give you something for the pain in just a couple of minutes." The nurse is very gentle and tries to inflict as little pain and discomfort as possible.

Ann calms down; she can feel her breathing slow and become deep and regular. She hears the machines as they continue to monitor her every breath. She could feel as the drug starts to take effect. She has no idea drugs could work as fast as they do.

The nurse went on. "You sure have a wonderful family. Everyone here just loves your daughter, and your son gives all our hearts a flutter when he brings out those big smiles of his. Your husband is a gem, too. You're one lucky lady."

Ann tries to talk, but her mouth is so dry. "Can I have some water, please."

"Of course. Let me get you an ice cube. It will work better for you, and you will not have to move."

With that, the nurse pops an ice cube in Ann's mouth. She has no idea that an ice cube could be so refreshing and desirable.

Ann relaxes and watches the nurse as she moves about the room, checking the machines and tubes going in and out of Ann's body. She tells Ann that tomorrow they may be able to remove her catheter tube and small drainage tube. The nurse's voice is very soothing, and Ann feels herself slip back in time again. She found herself entering a set of hospital doors, only she is not alone. Ed is with her, along with Jake, but Jake is just little.

Chapter Ten

Ed and Ann followed Nurse Doreen and Jake as they entered into the neonatal intensive care unit. Amy was in a small room off to one side. She's being cuddled by an older woman, to whom Doreen spoke. "Karen, this is Amy's big brother, Jake, and her new mom and dad, Ed and Ann."

"Pleased to meet you." Karen was busy wrapping Amy in a bright pink blanket. She pulled a pink cap over her head. "Your little sister does not like to have a bare head. She has a fine set of lungs and has been exercising them for us."

"Can I hold her?" asked Jake. "I washed my hands and everything." He climbed into a chair that was sitting to one side and patted his lap.

"Sure thing," laughed Karen. "She is hungry and will be looking for something to eat pretty soon. We have to teach her to drink from a bottle, so she may not sit very nice right now."

"That's OK. I'm getting hungry myself. Maybe she would like some tomato soup and grilled cheese sandwiches with me—that's my favourite."

Ann smiled. "No, I think Amy would like some warm milk in a bottle, but we can go have something to eat in just a few minutes. Now that you mention it, I'm a little hungry myself."

Karen lets Jake hold the new baby, while Doreen brings Ed and Ann up to date with Amy's condition. "She's very strong and a good size. The paediatrician will be here shortly to provide you with a full report, but for now, all tests indicate she can go home with no problems. She will probably stay a day or two just to be sure. Doctor Fritz will talk to you in just a couple of minutes."

Ed got down on his knees in front of Jake to admire the new baby. "I wish I had a camera to take a picture. This is the most beautiful sight a man can witness: not one life but two, ready to move forward, with an expectation of protection and love. Look at these two. Are they the most beautiful children you have ever seen?"

Ann had to agree and bent down to admire the scene from ground level.

Just then, a flash went off. Ann and Ed turned and discovered Doreen with a camera. "We take pictures of the new babies every day for our reports. I will send you a couple of pictures for your albums. Let's get a couple of shots of all of you and then some of just the children."

Suddenly, everyone was focused on taking pictures of this new little family.

"But we look like wrecks!" complained Ann. "I have no makeup on, and my hair hasn't been combed since … I'm not sure when!"

"You look fine. I think you're the most beautiful woman in the world, so smile nice for the camera." Ed moved beside Ann and put his arms around her and Jake.

"Now, everyone say cheese."

"My turn," said Ed to Jake, and he picked up the tiny bundle and held her close. Doreen snapped another picture. "Thank you, God," he prayed, "for answering our prayers and delivering this wee one into our lives. Help us to be good parents."

"Excuse me. My name is Dan Fritz." A distinguished grey-haired doctor with a crisp white hospital jacket put his hand out to Ann and then to Ed. "Can I take a couple of minutes to give you an update on little baby girl Green's condition?"

He led the family over to a small sitting area. "As you know, Mrs. Green was in critical condition, and we had to remove the baby quickly. The baby is approximately three weeks premature, but she has a good weight, since she's just over the five pounds—five pounds two ounces to be exact. Her lungs are fully developed and strong, and she has a good heart and steady pressure. However, due to the trauma her mother received while the baby was still in the womb, we would like to keep an eye on her and to run a few tests."

Ann and Ed nodded in understanding.

He went on. "I would like to keep her here in the NICU to monitor her. Once we get the test results, if all things remain as they are now, you can take her home. Do you have any questions?"

"We have had a really bad day, so can we think about that answer? We'll probably have lots of questions, but right now, we have to deal with so many issues, and quite frankly, we're exhausted," Ed answered for both of them.

The doctor nodded. "Unfortunately, you still have a couple of things to deal with before you can leave. They need you back at the trauma unit, since they have kept Mrs. Green on life support until all the paperwork is completed regarding the organ transplants. In fact, Mrs. Fletcher is waiting at the nurses' station for you now."

Just then, Nurse Karen appeared with a bottle for Amy. "Would you like to feed her?" she asked Ann.

"I would love to, but Mrs. Fletcher needs to see us. Can she wait a little longer?" Ann wanted to hold this little one, but Ed hadn't seemed to want to let go of her.

"Here you are, sweetheart. I didn't mean to hold her so long, but she just seemed to snuggle down in my arm." Ed adjusted the little bundle, who was now starting to squirm. Almost right on cue, she let out a cry. "I think she wants some lunch."

Jake pulled on Ed's arm. "I'm hungry, and I need to pee."

Ann took the baby, and Ed went off with Jake to find the closest bathroom. Karen led Ann to a rocking chair, where she sat down. She had no idea she was so tired, but sitting there in the soft light made her aware of the exhaustion and gave her a few minutes to take in all that had happened.

"Can I trouble you for a moment while you feed the baby?" A tall, red-headed lady extended her hand. "My name is Jane Fletcher, and I'm the organ transplant representative at the hospital. You need to know we have Mrs. Green on life support to ensure her organs continue to function until we can complete the necessary paperwork."

Jane stopped talking as she watched the nurse hand Ann the bottle and Ann struggle to get the baby to suck on it. Since Jane had five children of her own, she knew this was not always as easy as it often looked, especially with a preemie. "Just take your time. She will figure it out if you relax." She sat down on the footstool next to Ann. "I have five kids, so I know each one is different. This little one will figure it out soon enough."

Just then, Amy grabbed the nipple and started to suck. She choked, and Ann took the bottle out and put Amy on her shoulder.

"You're going to be a great mother. You did exactly the right thing," Jane said.

Karen was close at hand, just in case any problems arose. "Mrs. Fletcher is right. She may have to try a couple of times, but the baby's hungry and has been sucking her hand, so we know she has the sucking instinct. Try again."

Ann tried again, and Amy took the bottle. This time she swallowed. "Do you mind if we wait for Ed to come back before we talk about Mary?"

"No problem. In fact, we'll see if Doreen will take Jake for a few minutes so we can handle all of the legal issues. He's small and will probably not remember, but I need to be sure you understand everything so we have no problems." Jane knew this was hard, but she also knew from her day-to-day experiences that there was no easy way to handle these stressful situations. She knew how many lives would be saved with the organs they would collect from Mary. Two people were waiting for cornea transplants, two more for kidneys, one for the liver, and the heart was in good enough shape, it was being used as well. Several prayers were answered today, but it was unfortunate that such a vibrant life was lost.

Ann stared down at Amy. Ann had so many things to think about, and everything was coming at her at once. She closed her eyes and asked for guidance and strength to finish the tasks she had to handle yet tonight and into tomorrow. She felt her strength come to her as an answer to her prayer. She opened her eyes to see Amy watching her as she drank her formula.

Ann saw her beautiful blue eyes. Her flaming red hair was peeking out from under the pink cap. "She's going to be such a beautiful girl when she grows up. Look at that hair. She looks like a miniature Anne of Green Gables, doesn't she?" Ann looked up at Mrs. Fletcher, who nodded.

Both women sat in silence as Ann finished feeding Amy. They all had their own thoughts to keep them quiet.

"Wow, look at her eat. She takes after her father, doesn't she?" Ed had appeared out of nowhere, and both Ann and Jane were startled by his sudden appearance.

"Doreen has taken Jake to the nurses' station for some cookies to tide him over for a few minutes." Ed pulled up a chair next to Ann.

He put out his hand to shake Jane's. "My name is Ed Murray."

"Thank you for meeting with me tonight," Jane said. "I know this has been a long day, but we have a few legal formalities we have to complete before you can leave." Jane shifted in her chair. "Do you mind if we just sit here, or would you like to go to my office?"

"Here is fine," both Ann and Ed spoke at the same time. They smiled at each other. They had been together so long they could finish each other's sentences, and often did.

"If you don't mind, we are both very tired, and Jake needs to get some food and sleep."

Since Mrs. Fletcher had all the necessary documents with her, they quickly went over the paperwork, signed the pages, and headed for the nurses' station to collect Jake.

Chapter Eleven

Jake was happy to get his fries at MacDonald's and sat in his car seat, munching away on his cheeseburger and fries.

"We need to start a list of what we need to outfit our house and two new children." Ann got her notebook out of her purse to start a list. Ed drove as they made the list, periodically asking Jake for his advice on what he would like in his new room. They were both exhausted, but the list brought new energy, as they began to realize the expansion of their little family. They would go shopping tomorrow, after they went to the hospital to check on Amy.

The next list made them both very sad. They began to discuss the plans for the two funerals. "We'll bury them side by side, right here in Riverside," said Ed, taking charge of this difficult task.

"Yes, with yellow roses and white tulips for flowers. They were Mary's favourite, and Jeff brought her bouquets every time he came home from work."

"We'll call Pastor Ron in the morning and start making plans." Ed took his eyes off the road for a second to check on Jake. "Our little boy is sound to sleep. He has had one awful day."

"But he has not reacted too badly so far. I think we need help to explain everything to both children. We can discuss that with Pastor Ron. Actually, just Jake for now, but we have to always be honest with both of them. Amy will need to know in time about Mary and Jeff."

"We are going to need help with a lot of things; parents with two children in one day. God has a lot of faith in us."

"No kidding, I just pray we don't disappoint anyone. How will we handle it all? I will need to speak with Stewart and see about getting time off. I'm not sure I will be able to handle work and two babies. We are going to need to sit down and look at our finances. I'm pretty sure we can draw off the holiday funds to buy everything the kids will need to get us started. With no mortgage, we should be able to live off your salary."

"Well, I do have a few more years before I was planning to retire. Maybe I just add a couple of extra years."

"There are lots of people with kids, so if they can afford it, we should be able to handle, too. I'm sure God will make sure the kids have everything they'll need."

With that, Ed drove up to the garage and opened the door. "Here we are, home safe and sound. But it looks like I will need to leave the car outside tonight," as he stared at the sight of his once-clean, uncluttered, everything in its place garage. There were boxes everywhere, all neatly labelled but stacked everywhere.

"I guess we have more work, going through everything to decide what to keep and what to get rid of."

"Right now, I just want to get Jake to bed, have a warm shower, and go to bed," Ann said. "I feel like I have been up for several days. My eyes are full of tear salt, my face feels like I have spent a day at the ocean, and I'm weary to the bone."

Ed unbuckled Jake from his seatbelt and lifted him up over his shoulder. Jake opened his eyes, muttered a few words, and went right back to sleep.

Ann walked ahead to turn on the porch light. She saw a note on the door as she went to open it. It was from Bruce and Connie. She read it out loud. "Finnegan is going to be fine; Dr. Dave is keeping him until you're settled and ready for him. We'll be over by eight tomorrow morning. Don't make plans for breakfast; we have taken care of that. Try to get some sleep. See you in the morning."

"It is good to have friends like we have, isn't it?" Ann whispered as she motioned for Ed as he went through the door in front of Ann.

Ann went to the spare room, where Jake always stayed. "I guess this will be Jake's room. We'll need more kid-friendly furniture. We'll need to take the big truck into the city tomorrow. It may take a couple of loads to get everything we need for both Jake and Amy."

"That can wait until tomorrow. Now, I just want to say my prayers and head to sleep. I'm like you, absolutely exhausted."

Ann took off Jake's shoes and socks and folded down the covers so Ed could deposit the little boy in the big queen-sized bed.

Ann went to their ensuite bathroom, dropped her clothes, and headed into the shower. She noticed someone had tidied up the bathroom. She looked around and saw the bedroom had also been cleaned up. Connie must have come in and done a quick clean for her. She had to remember to thank her when they met up for breakfast.

Chapter Twelve

"Can we bring Finnegan home today?" Jake climbed up the side of the king-sized bed and jumped on top of Ed.

"Take it easy on an old man," laughed Ed, and he leaned over and helped Jake find a spot between him and Ann, depositing a kiss on Ann as he did so.

"Time to get up, we have to go get Finnegan. I'm hungry. Can I have some pancakes?"

"Let's get dressed and then we can have something to eat." Ann reached over and gave Jake a hug. "Did you have a good sleep?"

"Yep, and now I'm really really hungry for pancakes." Jake emphasised the really just in case they missed how hungry he was.

"OK, let's get moving. We have a busy day." Ann climbed out of bed. "I have a list of things we need to do, and we have company coming in just a few minutes."

Right at eight, the doorbell rang, and Jake went running to the door. He swung it open and announced company was here, so now pancakes could be made.

"Well little buddy, we are going to the pancake house for breakfast." Bruce picked him out and held him high over head. Jake squealed in delight. Bruce set him back on the floor.

Bruce and Connie didn't get time to talk, as Jake was pulling their hands to get to the pancake house because he was starving.

Once they had ordered their breakfast and everyone had coffee, Ann and Ed went over their list with Bruce and Connie. Jake had ordered pop, but he was satisfied with his apple juice. Everyone in the restaurant passed by

Ann and Ed and patted Jake on the head. All were close to tears, as they had already heard the news about Mary and Jeff.

Mayor Brian Windsor came to their table and passed an envelope over to Ed. "I have been busy answering requests to help you folks out," he said as Ed looked puzzled at this large stuffed envelope. "This will help out with your needs for the kids. There is also a gift certificate waiting at Wal-Mart and another one at Sears, both at the mall. Just go to the office once you get there. Let me know if you need anything else. I have asked the local banks to set up trust accounts for both children. You can drop by the banks some time next week, when things settle down. In the meantime, I'm now just telling people to stop there instead of my office. I'm even getting calls from outside the province. I guess the story about Mary and Jeff hit the news last night."

Ed passed the envelope to Ann. She didn't count the money, but the envelope was full of twenty, fifty, and hundred dollar bills. "I don't know what to say." Ed's eyes swelled with tears. "How do we begin to thank everyone?"

"You don't. You just do the best job you can with these two kids. Like they say, it takes a community to raise a child, and that is what this community plans to do for Jake and his new little sister." With that, the mayor shook Ed's hand, gave Ann a hug, and went on to the next table. After all, there was an election in the fall, and the mayor still had a lot of work he wanted to get done in his long-term plan for the town. "Every vote counts," was his motto.

Jake had finished eating and was clearly bored. "Let's go back to the house, so Jake can play with his toys while we split up that list of yours, Ann." Connie was already standing. "We'll need to set up some appointments and things. By the way, Finnegan can come home today as well. Dr. Dave called us just before we left the house to let you know. Why don't we drop by his office and pick up the dog while you get Jake busy?"

Once they were all back at the house and Finnegan was resting, Jake went out to play in his sandbox. Ann called the funeral home to make arrangements for Mary and Jeff to be taken there. She made an appointment for Ken Switzer, the funeral director, to drop by the house later in the evening, after Jake was in bed. Ann didn't want to leave Jake, and she thought it best to make the arrangements quickly so she had answers for Jake. She knew Jake would soon be asking questions—and by his nature, lots of questions.

It was decided that Ed, Ann, and Jake would go back to the mall. Bruce and Connie would meet them there. They would split up and get the things on the list. They would need to pick up a car seat to bring Amy home.

They had been surprised when Dr. Fritz had called to tell them earlier in the day they could check Amy out of the hospital after three that afternoon. He had ordered a couple of tests, and they had come back normal. Amy had taken to the bottle and was declared a healthy little girl, ready to go home.

Since they needed to know for sure how much money they would need, Ann called Wal-Mart and Sears. She was amazed to hear there was more than enough to buy everything she needed and more. They hit Sears first and then Wal-Mart. They filled the carts and had all the big items taken directly to Bruce's brother's big farm truck. Once they filled the big truck, Connie and Bruce head straight back to the house, leaving Ed and Ann to load the other items into the backseat and the trunk of Ann's car.

Ed's neighbours and friends Bert along with his wife, Cheryl and Al and his wife Joyce were watching for Bruce and Connie and started right in to unload the truck as soon as it arrived. Once the truck was unloaded the boxes were divided up and everyone started putting the furniture together.

Meanwhile, Ed and Ann picked up Amy at the hospital, and the two little ones sat side by side in the backseat. Jake watched his little sister sleep until they got home. Finnegan was at the door to welcome them; he was starting to look better already.

While Ed and Ann were busy learning how to release the seatbelt and take the car seat out of its holder without waking Amy up, Jake unbuckled himself and raced into the house. He shouted from the door that they should come see his new room, because he has a car he could sleep in.

Ed and Ann finally got the car seat out and carried Amy into the house. Everything had been unloaded, and everyone was busy putting things together. Connie had already started to wash all the clothes and bedding. She had even found time to fry up a chicken and had the rest of dinner ready.

"We took the beds out of two of the spare rooms and put them downstairs in your storage area for now. Hope that is where you wanted them." Bruce had stopped his latest job, putting the swing together. "I have the furniture set up in Jake's room, and Connie has made up the bed for Jake. The crib is in the first room, along with the other baby stuff. Boy, I forgot how much work these things are. Did you notice everything came in flat boxes?"

"Yeh, I owe you big time for this." Ed went on, "You guys must have really rushed to get this done."

"Not really. Bert and Cheryl and Al and Joyce dropped by, so we put them to work as well. That's why it looks so professional; Cheryl used her designer talents to set up the rooms," Connie laughed. "You would have known if I have done it: I would have just piled everything in rows."

Cheryl was the youngest of the friends and had found many couples were willing to hire her to help them design their homes. Ann, Connie, and Joyce loved her energy and enthusiasm and never really paid much attention to age. The four had become friends almost immediately on meeting as soon as they realized each one was building a house on the same street at the same time. They used to bring their lunch and sit under a nearby tree to watch the construction. Cheryl had given the others some fabulous ideas, which they had incorporated into their homes. Ann to this day loved her kitchen island and her tile in the bathrooms, all suggested by Cheryl.

Jake dragged them into his new room. They had purchased a car shaped bed for him, with the bedding and remaining furniture to match. The old guest room was now all decked out and looked very much like it belonged to a little boy who loved cars and trucks. They had even put up the wallpaper and trim, along with a road map rug. All in all, it was quite a change, and Jake was elated.

Jake immediately pulled out his toys, and Al and Bert, deciding it was time for a break, were setting up the pieces on the road rug. Ann chuckled as she watched the grown men play demolition derby with Jake's Matchbox cars.

After handing Amy to Cheryl, Ann wandered around her house. She couldn't believe her eyes, as she viewed all the flower arrangements that had already come to the house. They filled every room. "What are we going to do with all these flowers?"

"I called all the local flower shops and asked them to not deliver any more right now. They wanted to know what to do with the orders they already had. I told them you would call them tomorrow morning with the answer," said Connie as she wiped her hands on one of Ann's aprons.

"Maybe we should send flowers to all the nurses and other people who have been so kind to us." Ed looked around at all the arrangements. The cards from the flowers, along with other cards, were stacked in a little basket on the kitchen island. "The flower shops just need to send us the cards and messages and readdress the arrangements with just a simple thank you and God bless."

"Good idea. I will call the shops first thing in the morning." Ann continued to look around her house. She didn't recognize it with all the children's toy and high chairs, a double stroller, and other things strategically set out throughout the rooms. "It looks like this is a house full of kids. It is what I had always dreamed it would look like. After all these years, our house finally looks like a home full of love and family."

Connie announced dinner was ready, everyone sat down together at the dining room table, Joyce had fed Amy and she was cuddled down in the little swinging cradle next to the fire place in the living room. Jake refused to use his booster seat and was offended when Al suggested using the new highchair.

With heads bowed, Ed said grace and thanked God for the family and friends gathered together and asked for direction as they face the rest of the week.

The meal was great and it was not long before all the plates were filled and then emptied. Connie had made a banana cream pie, Jakes favourite.

Everyone sat back and enjoyed a time of fellowship. Al and Bert entertained with the challenges of putting the children's furniture together. The women moved to the kitchen to tidy up. Ann smiled as she watched her friends and family working together. She loved these special moments and she knew they would have lots of great times yet to come. She also knew there would be more tears before the week

Chapter Thirteen

Later in the evening, Pastor Ron Richards came over with Ken Switzer to help with the funeral arrangements. There would be a joint funeral, as Mary and Jeff would have wanted it that way. Pastor Ron warned them it couldn't be in the church, since the church would never be big enough; he knew everyone in town would want to be there. Fortunately, Ken had already started the plans that were necessary, and the town had made available its big multipurpose room. The local church ladies took over the job of providing lunch. The Christmas Cantata Community Choir was brought back together to provide the music for the service.

The remainder of the week had gone by in a haze, with so many people dropping by. Not to mention the fact that both Ed and Ann were exhausted from the attention that was necessary with a newborn and an active three-year-old. Jake kept busy entertaining the drop-bys and checking out all the new furniture, toys, and clothes that filled his and Amy's drawers and rooms and the backyard.

Ann's next memories were of the day of the funeral. Two oak caskets sat side by side at the front of the hall. Flowers lined the hall's stage. Yellow roses covered the caskets. Pastor Ron did an amazing job with the service, and several songs, all favourites of Jeff and Mary, were sung by the local singing group. The ladies from all the churches pitched in and handled the luncheon served after the funeral.

The following Monday, Ed and Ann met with Ann's boss, James Stewart, to get work started on the estate. There was a lot of work, since they had to deal with several issues and insurance companies. It seemed the in addition to Jeff's insurance policy at work, he and Mary held other policies to ensure their children would be amply taken care of should anything happen to both of them. They had also inherited money from their parents' estates.

It appeared the children would enjoy a very comfortable future, and it wouldn't be as stressful as Ed and Ann had anticipated.

It also seemed the estate for Jeff's parents, Jacob and Elizabeth, was not yet settled. Several rented storage units held furniture, pictures, and dinnerware that was supposed to be shipped to Alberta. Jeff and Mary had never gotten around to finishing the work. Ed and Ann made arrangements to have the contents of the units shipped to Alberta. They rented air-controlled units in Calgary to hold the items. Both felt strongly that Amy and Jake would someday truly appreciate these things from their grandparents.

Ed and Ann also started the legal adoption process that was necessary for them to fulfill the last wishes of Jeff and Mary. James explained both the settling of the estates and insurances, along with the adoption, would take several weeks and maybe even months, but he would do his best to speed things up. His brother, the doctor, had just delivered twins to the local judge. This judge loved putting families together through adoptions so James was confident the judge would move quickly to settle both the estates and the adoptions. Once all the paperwork was complete, James would have them come in to sign all the papers.

The hardest part of that day was telling James that she wouldn't be coming back to work, because the care of two small children was truly a full-time job. Jean and James had discussed this issue and knew it was the only choice Ann could make. They also knew they would miss Ann, as she was a valuable asset to their office and a great member of their team. James could see from the dark shadows under Ann's eyes that the events of the past few days had taken their toll. He could also see the joy and love shining in Ed's and Ann's eyes as they regaled him with some of the events that had taken place with Jake and Amy. They had already turned into proud parents.

Chapter Fourteen

Ann and Ed stood in front of a large oak desk in the judge's chambers, Ed holding Jake and Ann carrying Amy. The couple had invited their family, Ann's sister and her family and Ed's brother and his wife and son. Both families had visited several times during the past several months and loved the changes they had seen. Ann and Ed seemed to take to parenthood like ducks to water.

Ed and Ann had their friends Connie and Bruce, Joyce and Al, and Bert and Cheryl join their families, as the judge handled the ceremony to grant Ann and Ed legal custody of the two children. When he was finished, Jake announced that he could now call Ann and Ed by their real names, Mom and Dad, just as his real mother had told him to.

From the courthouse, everyone went to the church, where the baptism service for both children was held. Connie and Bruce were Jake's godparents, and Ed's brother, Owen, and Ann's sister, Katherine, were Amy's godparents. Amy cried as Pastor Ron sprinkled the water on her head. Jake just brushed the water off his head, flashing a look of annoyance at his parents. "You know I have my best suit on, don't you, Pastor Ron? You spilt your cup of water all over me." Jake's little voice echoed through the church, and everyone in attendance laughed and clapped.

"As you can see, Ed and Ann, you will not be alone in raising these two beautiful children. God will always be with you and your family, and the entire community is beside you to help you out. Don't be shy to ask for help. Each of us here today is available; you just need to ask." Pastor Ron finished the service and ended in prayer.

Ed and Ann decided to use these two events as a thank you to the community and to introduce Amy to the people who hadn't dropped by to see the baby girl. Public announcements had been posted in the local paper as well as played on the radio stations. Ann had the local baker design a three-tiered cake: one tier in Jake's favourite chocolate, the second tier in Ed's favourite carrot cake, and the top tier in her favourite vanilla. The baker amazed everyone with an incredible cake. Tiny angels in pastel pinks and blues adorned the bottom. The second tier was completely in blue accents, with little dump trucks and toys surrounding it. Jake's name was spelled out in building blocks that were made out of chocolate. The top was pink and white, with tiny bottles and shoes scattered around to remind everyone that little girls are made of sugar and spice. Amy's name was spelled out in rattles placed in the centre, directly above Jake's name. The baker also made several flat cakes to ensure everyone would have a piece of cake.

Ed had surprised everyone by arranging for clowns and a musical program as entertainment. There were games for the kids and local musicians so everyone could participate in the fun. Ann had hired the local caterer to serve beef on a bun, hot dogs for the kids, and lots of salads and desserts. There was plenty of food for everyone, with second helpings encouraged. She had also hired a photographer to make sure there were plenty of memories for everyone.

Everyone had a great time. The local newspaper and radio station covered the event, and to Ann's surprise, the local television station sent a crew to film the event for the news at 6 p.m. Ann was able to get a copy of the film to put away for the children.

It was a fun time. Ed did an amazing job delivering a speech, thanking everyone for helping out during the disaster and for being part of their lives. She saw the mayor dab his eyes when Ed talked about how important this town was to his family and how he would make a promise to ensure the children learned the importance of the community and volunteering.

At the end of the day, Ed and Ann put their children to bed and collapsed on the couch to watch the late news and see the events as had been recorded. Since their families lived close by, everyone had gone home, and the house was quiet.

Ann thought back over the day, and a few tears fell as she reflected over the past weeks. Though time does heal all, she continued to pray for the children's parents and her parents. She wished her parents and Ed's parents had lived to see this day, knowing that they, too, had suffered the loss of grandchildren at every miscarriage. She knew they were all watching from a distance and able to see all the love the children gave Ann and Ed. Ann thanked God that Ed had stood by her when she was convinced he would have been better off with someone who could bear children. God did answer her prayers, but at His time and according to His plan.

Today, they were legal parents, and with the estate and insurances finally settled, this chapter of their lives was complete. Even though they were both tired, Ann and Ed sat and talked about what the future held for them as they watched their children grow.

Chapter Fifteen

Ann feels someone squeeze her hand. She opens her eyes and looks up to see Ed, smiling down at her. She tries to raise herself, but the pain shoots through her chest as the muscles protest.

"Sweetheart, you're not strong enough to get up yet. Ann, lie back." Ed kisses her on the cheek. Ann shakes her head and holds onto Ed's hand.

The nurse comes in. "Good morning, Mrs. Murray. Did you have a good sleep?" Without waiting for an answer, she continued, "I'm your nurse for the day. My name is Maureen, and if you need anything, you just press this button and I will come. We have a bit of breakfast. I hope you will enjoy a liquid breakfast of juice, tea, and JELL-O."

Ed lets go of Ann's hand to leave, but she grabs it back. "It's OK. I will be right back."

"This is not going to take more than a couple of seconds, if you would like to just wait outside. I will call you right back in as soon as we are done here, and I'm sure you will want to spend some time with your wife."

Maureen removes the drainage tube from the side of her rib cage. Ann gasps in pain from the shock of the tube being removed so quickly. "It is easier to remove this in one quick movement. I know it hurts a bit, but it's a better way for you. We'll also take out the catheter. When we're done, I'll give you something for the pain. It's not as strong as you had last night, so if you think you need more, just push this button, and the medication will go into your drip." Maureen demonstrates the automatic medication dispenser unit on the side of her bed. "You don't have to worry about overmedicating yourself. Once you have reached your allotted amount, you can push it all you like and nothing will happen."

Ann nods and speaks softly, "Thank you. The drugs you gave me yesterday were pretty amazing. I had the best time; I was actually reliving my life. What day is it? How long have I have I been here?"

"You have been here five days; today is Wednesday. You collapsed on Friday afternoon at the office. I'm told that you had gone in to complete some forms that needed your signature from when you worked for James. Dr. Hammon had you rushed here by ambulance; they did surgery on you Monday, late afternoon. I guess you don't remember much?"

Ed was already back in the room and holding her hand. Ed doesn't let go of her hand but moves closer and kisses her, this time on the lips. "I thought I lost you," he says as tears fall onto her cheek.

"I don't remember much. A lot of pain, a bright light. Oh ,and I saw Mom and Dad, your mom and dad, and Jeff and Mary. They all looked happy. We talked for a while; they told me it was not my time. Next thing I remember was seeing you and the kids and lots of pain. I never knew I could hurt so much."

"Just take it easy. Amy tells me you're strong, and they're happy with how the surgery went. It is going to be some time before you're complete well and back to your old self, but she will give you details when she comes back after rounds. Jake will be in shortly. He was stopping at his office this morning to have one of his partners handle his appointments for today."

"How is the pain, do you need a squeeze of pain medicine?" Maureen asks. "Again, if you need anything just ring. I am right outside in the unit station." Maureen turns to leave, waiting just long enough to hear Ann's answer.

"No, I think it will be OK."

With Maureen gone, Ann continues. "The drugs they gave me before were something else; they took me right back to the tornado. I relived the whole thing, right up to the party after the adoptions were finished. Do you remember?" Ann smiles as she experiences the memories of the joy she felt as she and Ed rejoiced in their parenthood.

"I will never forget. As they say, it was the worst of times and best times for me. Marrying you was number one, but that day in the courthouse with the judge, when we officially became parents, was certainly the second-best thing that ever happened to me." He kisses Ann again. They hold hands and reminisce about the first days and weeks as parents. They discuss the plans they made back then and how the plans had materialized.

As the pain medication takes hold, Ann is able to relax and breathe easier. Maureen brings in a tray with some chicken broth, strawberry JELL-O, and tea. She has a straw so Ann can sip the food without moving. She puts the bed up a bit so Ann is more comfortable.

"Your doctor and daughter will be in shortly, Mrs. Murray. How is the pain?" Maureen checks the vitals, as they are continually tracked by the electronic equipment in the room.

"I'm fine, my throat still hurts but not as much. The pain in my chest is manageable," Ann replies as she sips her soup. "I never thought broth could taste so good."

"Not like your chicken soup, right, Mom?" Amy enters the room, walks over, and kisses her mother on the forehead.

Amy then checks the electronic equipment running in the corner to see what has been happening with her mother. She frowns a couple of times, but looks up to smile at both parents, who are watching her with concern.

"Is something wrong?" asks Ed.

"No, I think we may have a glitch in the system. We may have to run some tests later today or early tomorrow morning, but otherwise, things look fine." Amy does not want to lie to her parents, but until she checks out what she has just seen on the screen, she does not want to cause them any more stress than they already have with her mother's collapse and heart condition. She has to remember they can read her like a book, and she didn't realize she had frowned. She'd look at the data back in her office, where she's able to review the entire report from the time her mother was hooked up to the machines.

Amy tries to change the subject. "So, tell me, what have you been doing with yourself? I hear from the nurses you're an exemplary patient, with no temper tantrums or crying fits."

"Your mother and I were just reminiscing about the good old days. She tells me the drugs you gave her are not too shabby. I guess that's why people steal them." Ed sees what Amy's doing and hopes that Ann does not catch on. He plans to corner Amy in her office once Ann goes back to sleep.

"Jake called to tell me he would be in to see you in a little while. He wants to know if you need anything. Did you remember to bring Mom's books and glasses, Dad?"

"No, I thought it was too much of a temptation to bring her a book. You know how your mother gets when she starts reading and loses all track of time. Maybe just lying back and resting is a better plan—for at least today. I can bring those things tomorrow."

Ann hadn't noticed the facial interchange between father and daughter, but she agrees that reading is not something she feels like doing today. "Right now, eating soup is making me tired. I think holding a book would be exhausting. I can't remember when I have felt this out of sorts."

"Well, Mom, it's not every day someone opens your chest to check out your heart." Jake enters the room with a small teddy bear holding an even smaller angel. "They told me I couldn't bring flowers into your room, being ICU and all, but I found this little bear, and I thought you might like company when we're not around." Jake reaches over to drop a kiss on his mom's cheek.

"Hey, no tubes down your throat. That's got to make you feel better." Jake walks over and leans against the wall. "And you're eating. What the heck is that anyway?"

"Chicken soup with no vegetables, noodles, or meat. But, it tastes good, and I'll even have a bite of this JELL-O, even though I hate food that moves." His mother tries to laugh, but a shot of pain ends it quickly.

"You look better, Dad. You must have had some sleep, and a shower does wonders, doesn't it? I know I felt better just having some food and a couple of hours of shut-eye myself." Jake glances over at Amy.

"You always look good, Sis. I cannot believe some doctor has not snatched you up yet. I have never seen you look bad; unless you count the time I pushed you into the creek when we went fishing." Everyone laughed at that memory. Jake has a knack for putting people at ease. Even as a small child, he could make people laugh and feel better.

Ann gives her soupspoon to Ed and yawns. "I have pictures of that."

"Of course you do, Mrs. Kodak. You have pictures of everything we did," jokes Amy. "Yeah, we have good pictures and bad pictures. No one can ever say you didn't document our lives. You should have bought shares in the company when you bought Mom that first camera. Remember that, Dad?"

Amy's pager goes off. "Sorry, but I have to get back to work. Mom, I'll check in on you later. Dad, I'm sure I'll see you wandering the halls. Maybe you and Jake and I can meet up for an early supper—if you don't mind hospital cafeteria food."

"No way. I want you three to get a decent meal. There are plenty of nice places to eat around here, and Ed, I want you to take the kids someplace where you can sit down and enjoy your meal. Promise me." Ann looks into Ed's eyes. When she does that, she knows Ed would do it, just like he always did.

"OK, it's a date. We can meet downstairs by the main door; say at 4:00 p.m. I'll need to be back, since I'm on call this evening in the ER." Ann hugs her brother and father and gives her mom a kiss. "I love you all."

Amy left the room as her pager started to beep again. She hurries down the hall to emergency. It seems to be the day for heart attacks.

Ann lies back and listens as Ed and Jake talked about work and the weather. They start to plan for their next fishing trip. Relaxed, Ann closes her eyes and finds herself starting to drift back into the past.

Chapter Sixteen

"Mom, can I open a present yet?" Jake was on his hands and knees, counting presents under the Christmas tree. "I sure do have a lot of presents, don't I?" Ann had now been officially called mom by Jake for almost six months, but every time she heard the word, she had to give pause and thank God for her blessings.

"How do you know that?" Ann was watching from the kitchen, where she was making gingerbread cookies for the church Christmas concert.

"Well, everything in blue is mine, 'cause blue is for boys, and I figure all the stuff with Santa Claus on them is mine, too."

Ann laughed. "What about Amy? I'm pretty sure she has some presents as well."

"Seriously, Mom, can I open a present today?."

"Ten more sleeps and then you can open all of them. I think I hear Dad driving up the driveway. Maybe you can help him shovel the snow. He might even make a snowman for you if you ask really nicely."

Finnegan headed for the door, tail wagging. That signalled his father was indeed home, so Jake hurried to the back door to greet Ed. Ed barely made it through the door before he was engulfed from the knees down in a giant bear hug from Jake.

"Daddy, Daddy, I missed you," Jake exclaimed as he ran into Ed's knees. "Can we go out and make a snowman?"

"Let me come inside for a few minutes and then we can get you dressed up and do some man things together outside." Ed took off his winter coat and boots. He walked into the kitchen and planted a kiss on Ann's lips. "It sure is good to be home, and you smell good." Ed nuzzled Ann's ear. "It was one of those days at the plant. You know the kind that you can hardly wait to leave."

"You smell Mom's gingerbread cookies, and we can't have any 'cause they're for the Sunday school concert on Sunday." Jake proudly showed off his mother's handiwork. "See, I got to put the chocolate chips for buttons and raisins for eyes. Mom put white icing for their eyebrows and lips. See their little hands."

"Ah, can't we have a couple of broken cookies, please?" With a wink, Ed broke a cookie. "Look, this one here is no good, he has no head."

"All right, you can each have one. Now, out you go, or you'll ruin your appetite for dinner. It'll be ready in about an hour, so you better hurry. It takes you just about that long to get Jake's snowsuit on."

Ed and Jake went to the back entry and got out all the snow wear. Ed got the snow pants on Jake only to hear Jake tell him he had to go to the bathroom. Ann smiled as she heard Ed lecture Jake one more time about going to the bathroom before they start to get ready to go outside.

As she took the last cookie off the sheet, she heard Amy start to cry. *Perfect timing*, she thought as she started to heat Amy's bottle. She needed a quick sit while she fed the baby, as she had been on her feet all day making cookies and squares for Christmas Day and the church concert. This year would be special. She and Ed would be hosting both their families for Christmas dinner, and this year, as new parents, they would fully understand the joy of this special holiday season. She went into Amy's room. It was decorated in the beautiful teddy bear theme that her friend Cheryl had done when Amy first came home from the hospital. That already seemed like a distant memory, but it had been only five and a half months, almost six she reminded herself. She often felt a presence in the room, as well as in Jake's room. Ann knew it was Mary checking up on her. Ann often had one-sided conversations with her. Today was no exception, as Ann discussed with Mary the little outfits the kids would wear on Christmas Day. Ann had made matching red dresses for her and Amy. Of course, Amy's dress was full of ruffles and frills.

When she was in Jake's room, she would talk to Jeff and let him in on her dreams for Jake's future. Before they died, they talked about Jake becoming a doctor or lawyer, like his grandfather. Jeff had always thought his son might become a hockey player, but Mary, always the practical one, suggested he could do both with enough encouragement. They would laugh and compare Jake to Wayne Gretzky, the new player for the Edmonton Oilers. Jeff had nicknamed Jake "the small great one" after Wayne.

Amy smiled when she saw Ann enter the room. She was such a beautiful baby, always full of giggles and smiles. She had enormous dark blue eyes and reddish-blond hair like her father. Amy held out her arms for her mother and belly laughed as Ann blew on her tummy while she changed her diaper.

"Let's feed you while dinner finishes. Your father and brother will be in shortly, and they will be starved." Ann took Amy to the family room, sat down in the glider chair, and started to feed Amy. She discussed her plans for the menu and party games for Christmas dinner as Amy sucked down her bottle. As Ann was burping Amy, the door opened to loud noises. Sometimes Ed was as noisy, if not noisier, than Jake.

They had all adjusted to family life together. Jake still asked about his parents and Ed and Ann decided they would be open and upfront with both children and answer their questions. When Jake asked, they would get out the few pictures they had managed to find in the ditches after the tornado. Ann had put pictures together in photo albums. She had also cut out a newspaper story, asking for anyone who had pictures to allow her to print copies for the kids. She had been pleasantly surprised at how many people brought pictures. She also had taken the family picture she had taken of Jeff, Mary, and Jake just days before and framed it and put it on the wall in Jake's room. She was not sure what she would do for Amy, but she would handle that issue when Amy asked.

Later that night, as Ann was reading Jake his bedtime story, Jake interrupted. "Mom, can I tell you what Grandpa Jacob told me?"

"Jake, you can always tell me anything you want. What did Granddad Jacob tell you?" Ann was curious, since Jake hadn't even been born when his grandfather died. Ann remembered the first time Jake told her he had been with Granddad Jacob. It has been Granddad Jacob who had kept him dry and safe during the tornado. Ann had always wondered about that.

"Well, he thinks I should become a lawyer like he was. He told me about his work, and how he helped people move into their new homes."

Ann knew that Jacob had been the local lawyer and had handled real estate and estate work. He had disliked court proceedings and wouldn't do criminal work.

"So, do you and Granddad Jacob talk often?"

"We talk all the time, mostly when I'm here in my room, playing with my toys. He said I could skate, too, and that skating was fun. Can I get some skates and go skating?"

"Well, you're still pretty young. Maybe after the holidays we can look into buying skates." Ann knew Jeff wanted Jake to learn to skate, but he was so small yet, and Ann was concerned he might fall and hurt himself.

As if he were reading her mind, Jake rebutted her. "Mom, skating is good. The 'Great One' Wayne Gretzy never gets hurt. Zack and Alex play, so why can't I skate and play hockey." Zack and Alex were Ann's nephews. They had both skated from kindergarten and would be perfect to help her out with this.

"Well, let's talk to the boys when they're here for Christmas Day, shall we? Now, do you want me to finish this story?"

The next ten days passed quickly, with Ed's staff Christmas party, the church dinner, and the Christmas concert. Before she knew it, Ann was filling the Christmas stockings on Christmas Eve. All the gifts were neatly stacked around the tree. Although Ann never saw herself as having much talent when it came to decorating, she had worked hard to ensure all the decorations in the house were done as perfectly and looked as close to those in the magazines as possible. Cheryl had come over one afternoon to help her put some finishing touches on her place. Since Katherine, Ann's sister, was a floral designer, Ann spent a lot of time learning the fine art of decorating with flowers, ribbons, and bows. Her skills were showcased, as the tree blinked with almost one thousand lights, and every branch had flowers, bows, or ornaments. Ann stepped back to admire her work and adjusted one of the gifts. She had her Nativity Scenes set up in several rooms around the house.

Ed brought them each a simmering cup of Christmas tea. He set it on the coffee table, alongside the cookies and treats Jake had set out for Santa Claus. Even though their focus was on the birth of Christ, Ann wanted to share in the fun of Santa Claus.

Before Jake had gone to bed, Ed had told him the story of the birth of Christ one more time. Jake had played a shepherd in the church concert and had memorized the story. Using Ann's figurines, Jake was going to tell the story after dinner the next day. Ann and Ed had been surprised at how quickly he learned all the lines and scriptures.

Ann sat down on the couch beside Ed. She had turned down the lights, and the house was glowing in Christmas lights, the tree, and all the ornaments. Ann's father had been a real lover of Christmas, and together, she and her father decorated every room in their house, including the bathroom. When Ed found a small tree in each of the kids' rooms, he teased her about carrying traditions and decorating too far. "But that way, they will be less inclined to try to mess with my tree," laughed Ann.

Ed put his arm around Ann. "It sure is nice to have a little time to ourselves before the excitement of tomorrow hits. I love the kids with all my heart, but sometimes I miss spending time with my favourite girlfriend." He wrapped his arms around Ann and kissed her fully on the lips. It was a long and lingering kiss. "If I haven't told you lately, I love you with all my heart."

Ann moved closer and continued returned another kiss. "I love you, too."

"Would you mind if I gave you my present tonight, just the two of us?" Ed walked over to the tree and pulled a small box from one of the lower branches. "I hope you will like this?"

Ann looked at the little box. It was wrapped in gold paper and had tape covering the entire box. She looked at Ed with a puzzled expression. "Did Jake wrap this for you?"

"Nope, did it all by myself, and I'm extremely proud of the job I did. Look, it even has a small bow with ribbon," Ed boasted proudly.

Ann opened the box, and tears filled her eyes. Inside the box was a family ring, with a birthstone for each of the kids and him. "I put my stone in the middle and the kids on each side. Let me put it on your finger, just like I did when I asked you to marry me." Ed dropped to his knees in front of Ann. He took her right hand and slipped the ring on her finger. It was a perfect fit.

Ann spread her arms around Ed's neck and kissed him again. The weight of her body against him caused Ed to lose his balance, and they both fell over, laughing. Ed recovered, picked up Ann, and carried her to their bedroom. "What about the lights?" Ann mumbled. Neither of them cared, as they tumbled into bed together, sharing their love for each other.

They woke up hours later to Jake hollering for them to get up, that Santa had come. Amy was crying for breakfast. They shared a lingering kiss and hurried to spend their first Christmas together as parents.

Chapter Seventeen

The first two hours on Christmas day were complete chaos. Jake was amused by opening his stocking, while Amy was changed. Ed fed Amy her bottle to tide her over until breakfast. They opened their presents and sat back. Ann tried to take pictures of Jake as he opened his gifts. Jake loved his toys, but when a gift contained clothes, he quickly set it aside for the next one.

Amy was satisfied to play with the paper, as she sat propped up surrounded by pillows. Periodically, she would tumble over and then attempt to roll into the pile of wrapping paper, ribbons, and bows.

Ann always saved the boxes and ribbon and bows. Some of the boxes were recycled several years in a row. She spent hours wrapping and making the perfect ribbons and bows. Yet, here in only a matter of minutes, there were paper and boxes and ribbons and bows all over the room. This year, there were not many boxes worth saving after Jake tore into his gifts.

Jake was happy playing with his trucks, while Ed and Ann sat in the mess. "You clean up this room, while I put the turkey in the oven and start breakfast." Ann hauled herself up and bent down to pick up Amy. "I will stick her in the high chair with a teething cookie to hold her over just a little while longer."

"I will make the bacon and eggs as soon as Jake and I pick up the paper."

"Just remember to stack any salvageable boxes by the basement stairs. I would like to keep the boxes that are still in good shape." Ed smiled as he gathered up the boxes. When Ann turned her back, he slipped a few boxes into the garbage bag.

In no time, Ed had the bacon frying and the toast in the toaster. "Jake, go wash your hands, breakfast is almost ready." Ed inspected Jake's hands, and Jake climbed up to his chair.

"Perfect timing." Ann wiped her hands on her apron. "The turkey is in the oven."

They sat down together to eat breakfast. Jake bowed his head and said grace. At the end, he said, "Amen, let's eat." It was something that Jeff had always done, and Ann and Ed were surprised Jake remembered it.

Once breakfast was finished, they had lots to do. Company would be arriving shortly, so Ann lost no time in getting showered and dressed in her Christmas outfit, which matched Amy's little dress. She had made matching vests and ties for Jake and Ed. She had to remember to get her sister to take a picture of them before dinner, while the kids still looked presentable. She took a couple of minutes to add that to her list and crossed off the things she had already done.

Ann had put some Christmas music on the stereo, and the smells of turkey, ham, cabbage rolls, and fresh pumpkin pie filled the house. Ann had set the table in the dinning room the night before. She had made little napkin rings from paper towel rolls. The centerpiece contained three long white candles. Tiny crystal candleholders were placed down the table on either side of the big arrangement. She had made placemats and a runner for the table and sideboard. She had her mother's crystal Nativity Scene set in the middle of the table. Ann loved to set her table, and she was proud of the final results.

Finnegan let them know when their first guests, Katherine and her family, arrived. She had two boys and a girl. Carrie, the youngest, was just starting first grade. The boys, ten-year-old Alex and eight-year-old Zack, already played serious games of hockey. Jake occasionally watched them play and was excited to see them.

"Merry Christmas, everyone." Katherine had her hands full. Her husband, Bill, followed with a bouquet of red and white flowers. "Boy the house smells great. When do we eat?"

Katherine elbowed him. "You just ate breakfast. How can you be hungry?"

"I'm not. I just wanted to see what would happen." Laughing, he hugged Ann and shook hands with Jake and Ed.

"I want to hold the baby." Carrie took off her coat and boots and made straight for Amy, who was busy trying to put her new baby doll into her mouth.

Ann and Katherine headed for the kitchen with the goodies Katherine had brought. Bill and Ed went out to get the gifts from the car. Jake followed Alex and Zack downstairs.

As the men brought in their last load, Ed could be heard shouting at Owen, his brother. Owen had jumped out of the car, picked up a handful of snow, and pitched it at his big brother. Ed reciprocated with an even bigger handful of snow. Bill dropped the last gift inside the door and ran out to join in the snowball fight.

Sara, Owen's wife, came into the kitchen. "It is always good to see our husbands have grown up. I barely escaped a massive snow dunking." Laughing, she hugged Ann and Katherine. "Merry Christmas to both of you. Thank you for today. It's the first holiday without Trevor, and Owen and I are feeling a little old and a lot sad." Sara and Owen had only one child, Trevor. He was off at university in Texas, where he was majoring in oil and gas engineering design. "He has met a young lady from his class, and her parents invited him to join them in Little Rock, Arkansas. He seemed so happy and so excited, I couldn't say no to his request. We knew this day would eventually come, but I thought it would be later rather than sooner."

"We'll all face that eventually, Sara," declared Katherine. "I feel for you, because I know I'll have to face it three times over."

"Well, we have a whole new group of children to fuss over." Sara needed to change the subject; she had already shed a few tears earlier and was not going to let her loneliness for her son mess up Ed and Ann's first holiday as parents. "Now, where would you like these salads?"

"Let's see if we can find room in the fridge." Katherine took the biggest bowel and tried to find space. "On second thought, maybe we can store it out in the garage for a couple of hours."

"Make sure to check before you put your head out the door," Ann warned her, but it came too late as Sara shrieked as a cold, wet snowball caught her in the neck.

"Oops, sorry about that." Ed shook himself off. "I have things to do," he said as he ducked around the corner, looking sheepish.

"Let's head to the safe zone fellows, before we end up having to peel potatoes." Owen waved as he slipped around the corner, still covered in snow."

Ann had prepared as much as she could in advance, and the three women sat down for a cup of tea before dinner. They began to reminisce about Christmas with their parents. "Remember all the catering Mom used to do in the month of December?" Katherine sipped on her tea and snacked on a gingerbread man. "I was exhausted for a week after I cooked the first Christmas dinner after she died, and it was only for the six of us. I had a whole new respect for Mom."

"I know. I was thinking about that today as I was getting things ready. Do you remember the time we were working on a wedding just before Christmas at that small hall out in the Alder Flats area? Your job was to put cherries on the desserts." Ann loved this story; it was her favourite. "Mom told you to drain the cherries and make sure they were dry before they went on the whipped cream topping I had just piped on each fancy glass dish. You sucked the juice off each cherry."

"Yeah, Mom was really mad at me. Serves her right for not telling me to use a paper towel! I could never figure out how she got them so dry." Katherine laughed. "But, she never asked me to help with food again. She left me to decorating and setting it out. That was the best job."

"Was there a method to that?" asked Sara, enjoying the stories the two women told about their childhood.

"You bet, I got to do the things I enjoyed, arranging the flowers, setting up the buffet tables and putting the finishing touches on the tables. I never had to help in the kitchen. The problem is that Ann learned to cook and I didn't, still can't cook a good meal from scratch without a meticulous cook book with step by step directions."

The three women continued to share their stories and family tales as they finished their break and got back to the job of finishing Christmas dinner.

The house was full of laughter and giggles, as the children played together and the adults talked. Ann had always dreamed about holidays like this. This was the first year they had hosted Christmas. Usually, Sara and Katherine took turns hosting the holidays, since it was easier for Ann and Ed to travel because they had no children.

Once Christmas dinner was ready, everyone squeezed around the big dining room table. It was loaded with all their favourites. Since Ann and Katherine had been raised by a mother who was a caterer for many years, they knew how to prepare a fabulous meal with all the trimmings. Ann had always helped cook, and Katherine, with her artistic flare, was the specialist in presentation. Together, along with Sara, they had prepared a feast fit for royalty. Amy fell asleep just at the right time, giving Ann an opportunity to eat her meal without the little one fussing. In fact, Amy had proven herself a little angel and impressed everyone with her best Christmas Day behaviour.

As was their tradition, there was always an empty place set at the table in memory of those who were not with them. It had been a tradition passed down from Ann's grandmother. This year, that empty place held so much more meaning than just their parents. Katherine had made a miniature floral arrangement of white sweetheart roses and set it in front of the plate. Everyone held hands as Ed prayed. After grace, as always, Jake added, "Amen, let's eat."

Katherine and Sara looked at Ann, who explained, "His father always said that at the end of grace at every meal, and we've just let him continue." Everyone nodded in understanding.

It always amazed Ann. They spent hours preparing the food, and in no time, the bowls were emptied, and everyone was sitting back in their chairs, declaring they would never eat that much again and dessert should wait until after the gifts were opened.

After the men and boys cleared the dishes, they all went into the living room to open their gifts. Carrie had gone to get Amy, as Amy's perfectly timed nap was over. Ann appreciated how much help Carrie was. Jake sat patiently beside the tree. "I'm going to hand out all the presents to everyone," he proudly demonstrated with the first gift.

"I will help you." Carrie sat on the floor, with Amy on her lap and Jake beside her. "Amy can help, too."

"Amy only likes to eat paper," Jake tolerantly explained to Carrie. "She's just little and does not know about presents yet."

With everyone gathered in the living room around the tree, Jake began to hand out the presents. That is, until he got to his. He forgot about handing out the rest of the gifts. "Can I open my present now?"

Everyone answered together, "Jake, open your present." Jake tore off the paper and shouted with delight as he saw a picture of a pair of skates on the outside of the box. He quickly opened the box, and there were a brand new pair of skates, along with a second box that contained a hockey helmet.

"Can we go skating now?" Jake was trying to put on his skates.

"Not right now, little buddy. You have to wait to put the skates on at the skating rink, because they will cut up Mommy's hardwood floors." Ed exchanged the skates for the hockey helmet. "Let's try on the helmet instead."

Katherine had called everyone in advance to let them know she had bought Jake the skates and helmet, and she reminded everyone to bring their skates so they could go skating.

Ed had a surprise for all of them. He had been busy the last few nights, flooding the backyard with water for his homemade hockey rink. He had worked hard to make sure Jake did not go into the back yard, building snowmen only in the front and only shovelling the front sidewalk when Jake was around. Ann worked hard to help in the evenings after the children were asleep.

After everyone finished opening their gifts, they dressed up and went out to the backyard. Ann bundled up Amy and put her into her new little red wagon. Jake was so excited to get on his skates, and amazingly, they fit perfectly. Ann had not realized Katherine had measured Jake's feet the last time they were together.

Alex and Zack cruised around the rink and declared Uncle Ed had done a great job. As critics, they explained that while not as good as the flooded arenas they were used to playing in, it was a great place for them to start teaching Jake the finer art of hockey and skating. Katherine and Bill spent so much time at the arenas; they were used to putting on skates and were first on the ice. Bill was an assistant coach, so he could put on skates in record time. Ann was last on the ice. Owen and Ed were already racing around in circles. Living in Alberta, spending time on the ice was natural, and everyone knew how to skate.

Jake got on the ice and immediately landed on his butt. He looked up with a look of defeat on his face. Alex skated over and helped him up. "You know, I couldn't even stand up when I started. Mom had to pull me around the ice. I was so wet and cold from all the ice on my bottom. I thought I would never learn how to skate. But, if you practice every day, it won't be long before you can race Uncle Owen and your dad and beat both of them. They're old you know." Jake laughed and got up to try to make it around the rink without falling.

Jake got up and tried again and again and again. Pretty soon, he was moving between Alex and Zack. After an hour, everyone else went back into the house for hot chocolate and dessert. The boys stayed with Jake and kept him balanced. "Your boys are so good with him, Katherine. Thank you so much for that gift. Jake wanted skates, but I thought he was still too small. You proved me wrong." Ann hugged her sister.

"Well, you might as well come with us tomorrow to Airdrie for Zack's tournament. Amy needs to get used to a life on the bleachers. You'll be spending the next fifteen years or so eating and sleeping hockey. Jake is a natural. Look at him, he has taken a couple of real nasty falls, and yet, he just kept getting up and trying again. Every parent thinks their son is the next Wayne Gretzky, but you might really have a son who will make it all the way."

"I'm not sure that is what I want for Jake." Ann paused from cutting her famous chocolate lover's cheesecake. "I don't want him to get hurt. I was hoping for a doctor or lawyer."

"I will tell you what I tell my boys: play and have fun and when it is not fun anymore, stop. If you follow that rule, Jake will tell you when he has had enough."

"You're so right, Katherine, I have never forgiven my mother for not letting me play hockey," confessed Ed. "She wouldn't let Owen and I play, because she thought it was a terrible sport. We had to take piano lessons instead. Do you how badly we were teased at school. It was terrible. I want Jake to make his own decision. Who knows, maybe he'll try for a year and decide he wants to do something else. What do you think, Ann?"

"Since Jake is not even four yet, let's wait and see what happens. Do you want to call the boys in and let them have some hot chocolate? It is getting cold out there, and Alex and Zack are both playing hockey tomorrow." Ann put the mugs of hot chocolate on a tray. "Then, if you would be so kind, you can carry this downstairs for you and the guys." She passed the tray to Ed. The boys all went downstairs to watch a Christmas hockey game. They filled up on dessert and fruit and warmed up with hot cocoa and marshmallows.

Katherine, Bill, and their family left some time later. The house suddenly seemed quiet. Ann had taken Jake for a bath, and Sara was feeding Amy her night time bottle. Ed and Owen were talking about work.

"Mom, I had so much fun today. I wish Christmas came every day." Jake was playing with his toys in the bathtub full of bubbles.

"I'm glad you had a good time. You remember that today was Baby Jesus' birthday, right?"

"Yep, I sure do. Do you think Baby Jesus got skates like me?"

"No, I don't think so. Baby Jesus didn't grow up in Alberta. He lived where there was not much snow and no hockey rinks, just lots of sand and rocks."

"Mom, I want to play hockey like Alex and Zack. Is that OK with you and Dad?"

"Let's talk about that tomorrow at breakfast." Ann lifted Jake out of the tub, dried him off, and after a round of good nights and good night hugs and kisses; he went off to bed with no protest. In fact, he lay down and while Ann was finding his story for the night, he fell asleep.

Ann brushed his hair off his forehead and gently kissed him. "Good night, my little prince. Sweet dreams." She closed the door and went back to the living room for some quiet time with Owen, Sara, and Ed. Sara had fed Amy and rocked her gently to sleep. "Can I put her in her crib?" Sara asked Ann.

"By all means. If she's as tired as Jake, she might even sleep right through until seven tomorrow morning." Ed looked guilty at suggesting such a thought, but Ann nodded.

The four of them sat and drank tea Owen and Ed had made. As the two women talked, the men decided they were hungry and need a late night snack. Ed got out the leftovers, and they each made themselves a huge turkey sandwich. They sat together in the kitchen and discussed the events of the day.

Owen shared with Ed that their son, Trevor, was having dinner with his girlfriend in Little Rock. They discussed the fact that Owen and Sara's little boy was growing up. Owen talked about how hard it had been, especially for Sara, when Trevor announced he didn't want to be home with them for Christmas this year. The brothers regaled stories about their time spent at university and then laughed and joked at all the practical jokes and pranks they were involved in.

Sara and Ann had their own discussions about Trevor and his interest in finishing school in Texas. Ann saw the pain Sara had over the fact that her little boy was growing up and had spread his wings. Ann worried about how she would feel when Jake and Amy left home for university and their own lives.

After they finished their snacks, Owen and Sara headed home to call Trevor.

Later that evening, after they had tidied up the house, an exhausted Ann fell into bed next to Ed. "I'm so tired, but it was a great day. I really enjoyed having everyone at our house for a change. It was such a special day for me. I'm glad everyone had a good time."

"Are you kidding? It's a good thing my brother only lives an hour away. He would have stayed over. He and I had such a good time together with the boys and Bill. He was feeling a little down with Trevor not around."

"I know. Sara seemed to be a little distant every once in a while. Katherine cheered her up. It was a great day for me, as well. I think Jake loved it, too. He sure didn't complain about going to bed."

"Amy was such a perfect angel today. Can you believe it? Now no one will believe us when we complain."

"It was nice to have help. Carrie wants to come spend some time with us over the rest of the holidays. She's so good with the kids. Maybe we can let her spent a couple of nights. She has never spent the night away from home, so maybe this would be good for her. Let's talk to your sister tomorrow."

Ed put his arms around Ann and kissed her good night. Ann was already fast asleep.

Chapter Eighteen

Ann felt like she was floating as she watched the days go by, and it was not long before February 22 rolled around and Jake celebrated his fourth birthday. Ann had invited several children from Jake's Sunday school class. They were all together in a play group as well.

Ann spent hours putting together plans, party treats, and birthday decorations—with Jake's help. He was so excited to have a birthday. Ann wondered how long that would last, since her birthdays seem to come way too often for her liking.

Ann chose a Mickey Mouse theme, since Jake loved watching Mickey Mouse. He was waiting for his baby sister to grow up more so they could take a trip to meet Mickey in person. Ann and Jake made mouse ears for everyone, including Finnegan. Finnegan was not impressed, and his ears came off very quickly. Jake decided since Finnegan already had floppy Pluto ears, he didn't have to wear his Mickey Mouse ones.

Ann had decorated a Mickey Mouse cake and had found all sorts of fun games to play. She made Goofy hot dogs and Minnie Mouse chocolates. Ed took the day off so he could help out. It was a busy day for both of them, with all the extra little bodies running around the house. As usual, Finnegan followed Amy wherever she went to make sure he cleaned up whatever she couldn't or didn't have a chance to put in her mouth.

Ann felt herself moving forward through time. She could see all the activities as she saw herself go from one memory to another. Time was moving very quickly.

She saw herself at the cemetery, placing flowers in the holder at the headstone of Jeff and Mary. "I hope you're happy with how I'm doing at the job of mother." Ann talked to Jeff and Mary and prayed as she sat for a few minutes to talk to her friends. She often contemplated life and life issues when she did her stopovers at the cemetery.

Ann was a regular visitor at the cemetery. She made sure a trip to the cemetery was on her list for all the important dates, such as birthdays and holidays. Sometimes, she just slipped away for a few minutes when Ed was around to watch the kids. She knew that Ed often spent time there as well. When the weather was nice, she put the kids in the wagon and walked the short distance.

Often, Jake would ask questions, and Ann always took the time to explain the truth. As he grew older, she talked about Jeff and Mary and the fun times they had together. One day, Jake asked Ann if she missed her mom, to which Ann replied, "I think about her all the time, and I remember all the great fun things we did. I try to do those fun things with you, so you will remember the fun we have. That makes me smile."

"I talk to Mom a lot." Jake spoke very matter-of-factly about his parents. "She sure laughs a lot when I tell her stories about Amy and you and Dad. I like the sound of her laugh." Ann hugged Jake, as the lump in her throat didn't allow words to come forward.

Now, Ann found herself one year later, July 31, Amy's first birthday. The first year together had moved quickly. It was hard to believe Amy was already a year old. She walked around and was starting to form words. Jake pushed her to talk and refused to give her things if she didn't say the word correctly. Her first birthday had metamorphosed into a huge event, with the entire family and all their friends coming to help celebrate. Amy's list of play friends was nonexistent. Jake explained to his baby sister, "You're just little; you have no friends."

Despite having no friends her own age, the house was full of friends and family. Amy had her own cake, which she seemed to enjoy. As they sang happy birthday, Amy started to cry. Ann picked her up and held her as the cake was relit for another picture opportunity.

"One more time, Amy. You blow like this." Jake explained how to blow out the candles one more time. Apparently his little sister was a slow learner, since he had already showed her twice that day, with his father's assistance, how to blow out a candle. Amy finally figured out there was nothing to fear and went back into her high chair so she could eat her cake. Finnegan sat beside the high chair, hopeful that, as usual, most of Amy's food would come his way. Jake stood by his little sister as she stuck her finger in the cake and sampled a taste of icing. Amy was such a little lady.

Ann remembered the big first birthday party Mary and Jeff had for Jake. They had invited so many friends to share the special day. Mary had worked hard to decorate the cake and set up the house so everyone would have fun together. "What a difference between how you ate your first cake, Jake," Connie reminisced.

"Boy, is that right," said Bruce. "You put both hands into that cake and tried to shove the entire cake into your mouth in one bite. What a mess."

"Did I do that, Mom?" Jake looked at Ann in disbelief.

"You sure did." Ed laughed. "I remember watching your mom cleaning up the high chair. You went straight to the bathtub when you were done. You had a blue cake, and your face was blue for two days."

Alex poked at his brother. "Zack here had icing up his nose and in his ears. The dog was his best friend for the rest of the day."

"I have the picture Mom took of you in your birthday suit, with cake all over your fat belly." Zack pushed Alex over onto the grass. "Come on, Jake, let's tickle Alex." The backyard rang out with yelps and shrieks, as the boys rolled around on the grass and played on the trampoline.

Ann sat back and prayed that she would never forget the fun they had as a family.

Chapter Nineteen

There is a knock on Amy's office door. Her father and brother poke their heads in. "Are you busy or can we come in?" Jake asked.

Amy gets up and waves them in. She gives them a hug. "Sorry, I was supposed to meet you downstairs, wasn't I?"

Jake returned the hug and walked over to a big chair and dropped down in the chair. "That's OK. We thought maybe you might want to tell us something. I saw the look you had when you were checking the computer chart. Give it up, Sis. What's happening?"

"Dad, come and sit down." Amy walks over to her couch. "I can show you later, but I want to explain a few things."

Her father sits next to her and holds her hand as she talks. "As you know, every open heart surgery has potential for risk of complications that are specific to each procedure that is performed. Before and after the surgery, Mom's heart stopped. We were able to get it back both times.

During surgery, we stopped Mom's heart, and her blood was pumped by a cardiopulmonary bypass machine instead of her heart. This makes it easier for us to repair the damage and complete the valve repairs. I'm not sure why, but her heart has periodically slowed to an abnormal heart rhythm several times since then. I'm reviewing all the computer data. She may have suffered some damage to her heart tissue as a result of the lack of blood flow to the heart. This is very unusual, and doesn't usually occur with the new machines that have been developed over the past few years. Her irregular heart rhythm might simply indicate she needs either a temporary external or maybe even a permanent internal pacemaker. This can be inserted very easily, with minimal discomfort. We do these surgeries every day. Right now, we're monitoring Mom to make sure she has not developed a blood clot or cardiac tamponade."

"That one sounds bad. What exactly is cardiac tamponade?" Jake leans forward to ensure he takes in everything his sister is telling him.

"It is a condition where the pericardium, that's the sac surrounding the heart, fills with blood. It makes it difficult or impossible for the heart to function properly."

"That sounds dangerous?" Her father's frown grows deeper as moisture starts to develop in his eyes.

"I will not lie to you; it could be life threatening, but only if it's not handled quickly. If that happens, we're prepared to move immediately. Right now, we're watching for any change, even the slightest. I have asked Dr. Morgan to review the files and get back to me. I'm hoping it's just a case of needing a pacemaker, but I need to be sure. Because I'm personally involved, I need to have a second opinion. We should know by morning. For now, we're monitoring her on several computers, one with Dr. Morgan at his home office and mine here in the office and on my cell. I'm sure everything will be fine, but as a doctor, I have to look at all the possibilities, options, and directions her condition could take.

"Dad, I need to talk to Mom later tonight. I will explain everything I've just told you. I don't want to scare her, but every patient must legally be informed and understand their diagnosis and options, including any risks they may end up facing. I have to be sure she understands, and to protect me, I will bring one of my associates in to ensure Mom understands what I have told her."

Jake adds his two cents. "You have to make sure you're protected. I agree it would be better if you explained this without Dad and I there to confuse her. You know how she worries about everything."

"Exactly. So, if she knows what's happening, it will make things easier for her, and she'll not worry so much." Amy's relieved that Jake and her father understand what she has to do as a doctor.

"I agree its better she just relax and heal. I think if she understands everything, she can relax and not worry." Ed feels better as well. He's been concerned about what to tell Ann, since he knew she was already concerned about the attention the staff was giving to the monitors in her room.

"Now, let's go get something to eat. Mom's been drifting in and out of sleep most of the afternoon while we were sitting there. Dad and I have built up quite an appetite watching her rest." As usual, Jake's off-the-wall humour has lightened the mood.

"I'm not sure where you store all the food you eat, Son. You sure don't have my problem," Ed laughs as he pats his slightly rounded stomach.

"Hey, at least you're not as big as Uncle Owen. Now there is a man who needs to meet Jenny Craig." Jake teases good naturedly. He has always loved to tease his Uncle about his appetite and waist size.

Laughing, they get up to go and eat. As they walk out the door, Katherine and Bill meet them, along with Owen and Sara.

"Were your ears burning? We were just talking about you, Owen." Ed gives his brother a big hug and pulls on his hair.

"We went to see Ann, but she was sleeping. So, we thought we might find you up here." Katherine hugs Ed, Amy and Jake. "I know you have kept us updated by text, but we needed to see for ourselves how things are."

"Well, you're just in time to join us for some supper." Jake pulls his hand through his hair. "My treat!"

"Well, in that case, lobster here we come," Bill teases as he moves toward the door.

Just down the street from the hospital is the local Keg, a regular and favourite of both Jake and Amy. Jake often joins Amy after work for a bite to eat. Since they're both still single, they enjoy the opportunity to share their stories about the happenings of their days. It's the next best thing to eating supper with their parents at home. Even though they each own a house in the city, they still think of home as the house in Riverside, where their parents have lived for almost fifty years.

After they are seated and place their orders, Ed, with help from Amy, explains Ann's condition and prognosis. They share their stress and concerns. Ed tells them with over half of the town praying for her; it really is up to God to decide what will happen to Ann. He's sure she'll be home and sitting in her favourite chair very soon.

They spent the next few hours catching up on what Zack, Alex, Carrie, and Trevor have been doing. Alex, married with two children, is now an environmental engineer, working on several projects that take him all over the world. They live not far from Katherine and Bill. Zack has become the fireman he has always wanted to be and is stationed at Firehouse No. 51 on the southwest side of Calgary. He lives nearby, with his wife and three children. Carrie is happily married and works as a health safety environment coordinator at a local gas plant. She has two sets of twins and lives close to Katherine and Bill as well. Her husband is part owner of a small oil and gas company. Trevor is living in Little Rock, Arkansas. He's an architect, working in his father-in-law's architectural firm, alongside his wife. He switched his major from engineering to focus on architecture after spending his first Christmas with Heather and her family. He spent time in the office and realized he loved this line of work.

Owen and Sara continue to keep the mood light, as they begin regaling the tales of their time spent in Arkansas with their four grandchildren. They have just returned to Calgary, having caught the first flight available when they heard about Ann.

Amy sits back and just listens. She knows eventually the conversation will come to her and Jake and when they are going to settle down. No one realizes how hard she's had worked to complete her medical degrees and the long hours she spends in emergency and surgery. There are not many men who appreciate the eighteen-hour days she spends at the hospital. It's not that she hasn't tried to find someone to share her life with—she's not that fussy—but she looks at what her parents have and wants nothing less for herself.

Jake was engaged three years ago, but Andrea had died in a terrible car accident just weeks before their wedding. Jake never talks about it, but Amy knows he's not ready to try looking again. Jake is such a rugged, good-looking man, with his reddish-blond hair and big blue eyes. It's such a shame he can't move forward with his life. He loves kids; Amy sees that when he plays with their cousins and their kids. Amy knows her mom and dad are praying that Jake will find someone who can love him as much as they all do.

Amy's beeper goes off. She looks at the message. "Sorry, guys, I have to get back to the hospital, and no, it's not Mom." She sees the look of relief in her father's soft blue eyes.

"I do have other patients, but this one's just arriving, heart attack on way in from Strathmore." Amy gets up, hugs her aunts and uncles, gives her father a peck on the cheek, and messes up her brother's hair.

"Thanks for supper, Bro. My turn next time. Let's meet up again tomorrow night, if that works for you guys. I always enjoy your company, and Dad needs your support. Besides, we never get together enough and just have fun. Love you all."

Amy rushes out of the restaurant and down the street toward the emergency room. As she steps into the cool night air, she realises summer's in full swing. Fall is just around the corner. Soon, the leaves will start to turn, and the landscape will come alive with colours of gold and orange and red. She takes a deep breath and smells the flowers that line the street toward the hospital. She's always wished she could find a house for sale right there, but so far, her realtor-friend has not been successful in that quest. But, she did find a special house, which she just bought, a couple of developments further away. She moved in two weeks ago. She picks up the pace as her pager rings out again. She doesn't bother to look at it; she knows she's needed in emergency, since the Stars Air Ambulance helicopter must be landing with her patient. She uses her card to access the side door of the trauma unit and steps back into her world of life and death.

Chapter Twenty

Ann has fallen back to sleep, as the pain meds have once again taken over.

"Mom, are we ready for the tea party?" Amy asked as she finished seating all her guests. "We want real tea and everything."

Ann found herself in her backyard again, this time at Amy's sixth birthday party. The yard was full of balloons and bright paper and, of course, several little girls in pretty dresses with fancy and very funny hats. They had chosen a hat-themed birthday party. Ann had made a hat-shaped birthday cake in Amy's favourite shade of blue, with big, edible red and yellow roses. There were six roses, with a candle centered in each flower. Ann spent the better part of an afternoon getting the cake just perfect.

Ann laughed as she carried out the teapot, fancy cups, and saucers. It had been quite a chore to find all the fine china cups and saucers for the girls. She had so many china sets herself: her own grandmother was a stickler for tea served in china, and before she died, she gave her two granddaughters all her tea sets, including two silver tea services. Ann loved her tea service and enjoyed cleaning the silver. But, she was not ready for six six-year-old girls to use it. She wanted to leave Amy the sets in their entirety.

So, off to the thrift shop she and Amy went. It made the birthday preparations that much more special for both of them, and she hoped it would leave a lasting memory for Amy of their time together. They went to three thrift stores before Ann found what she was looking for. "Ohh," and, "Awe," came as she carried the out the fancy tray.

"You sure went to a lot of trouble this year, Ann." Her friend Connie was helping today. "Birthdays at my house are so boring when we compare them to your parties."

"I know, Connie, but I want to be sure Amy has lots of memories, and I know Mary would have spent all this time to make the perfect birthday."

"Ann, you need to learn to leave Mary in the past. She's gone, and you're Amy's mother."

"Connie, I know you think I'm nuts and need psychiatric help, but I feel Mary with me, watching over the children. The promise I made to her will be with me until my last breath. Besides, Amy and I had so much fun getting this ready. Making up the invitations kept her busy for hours. She printed every word herself."

Ann changed the subject, since she knew her friend did not agree with her relationship with Mary and could not figure out Ann's obsession with keeping her promises to her. It's been a bone of contention with her best friend. In Ann's mind, Connie just didn't understand.

"Now, if I could just keep either of my kids busy for that long on a single project, I might actually get my ironing caught up." Connie had taken the clue, and they got back to focus on the birthday. "Little girl parties are so much more fun than boys parties. You're so lucky Amy loves to be a little girl and didn't turn out to be a tomboy."

Both of them watched as the little girls all took their places at the big table. They were all dressed in their best dresses, little handbags, fancy hats, and white gloves. Ann was so pleased that the girls' mothers all took Amy's request to dress "formal" so seriously. Of course, Amy had to have a full explanation about formal wear, and they watched a rerun of Princess Diana's wedding so she could see how nicely the girls all dressed. Amy showed the movie to her friends and asked all the girls to wear fancy hats. Since they didn't have hats, Ann had a hat craft day for the girls and their mothers earlier in the month.

What fun they all had when they came over to work on their hats. They glued feathers and bows and ribbons and flowers. Ann remembered the fun she had with her grandmother. Her grandmother had come from a family of hat makers from England. Ann still had the hats that her grandmother had made, and they were truly works of art. Every outfit her mother and grandmother made for Ann came with a matching hat. Several were mother-daughter outfits. Ann remembered every grandmother, mother, and daughter matching outfit. Her mother kept Ann's many beautiful outfits, but unfortunately, it had never occurred to anyone that Ann might someday have a little girl and want her mother's matching outfits. Over the years, Ann made several trips to the fabric stores, and sometimes, she was lucky enough to find similar materials. She loved to sew and make her and Amy matching outfits for church. Ann would often make matching shirts for Ed and Jake as well.

Once the tea was all slurped, the fancy rolled cucumber sandwiches eaten, and the cake devoured, the girls played with their baby dolls. One by one, the girls left with their mothers. Finally, it was just Ann, Connie, and Amy left. "I can have one last cup of tea with you Amy and then I have to go home to make supper for the boys," said Connie as she poured a fresh cup of tea from a freshly brewed pot. "Thank you for inviting me. I enjoyed myself with just girls for a change."

"I'm glad you came. Mommy sometimes needs a friend, too." Amy spoke with so much experience in her tone.

Connie winked at Ann. "I love my hat. I think I should wear it to church on Sunday. What do you think?"

"We could start a whole new fifties trend at the church," Ann said, smiling. Sure enough, it was like an Easter parade Sunday morning, with all the girls wearing their hats.

Moving forward in time, Ann suddenly found herself on the steps of the entrance into the sanctuary of their church. Ann realized this was the twenty-fifth anniversary of her marriage to Ed. She was wearing the same wedding dress she had worn twenty-five years earlier. The difference was the man on her arm. An eager nine-year-old tugged at her arm. It was Jake, not her father, about to escort her down the aisle.

"Come on, Mom, the music has started. We have to go. Dad and Amy are already at the front."

Ann reached down and planted a kiss on his cheek. "Then let's not keep everyone waiting."

"Yep, let's get this show on the road." Ann sometimes wondered where Jake came up with these sayings—and then she remembered her husband and brother-in-law. Enough said, on with the show. As the music played, Ann remembered her dad's words to her before they started down the aisle, head up and shoulders back, look tall and proud, so she checked her shoulders and head and took hold of Jake's hand as they made their way down the aisle.

Pastor Ron stood with Ed and Amy. Ed looked so handsome in his new suit. The suit he wore twenty-five years ago hadn't fit properly, so Jake and Ed went shopping for new matching suits. Ed looked as full of love for Ann as she remembered all those years ago, on her first trip down the aisle at her parents' church. White and pink roses adorned the church. Katherine had brought the church to life with the vision of beauty and the smell of roses. She'd made a special white rose arrangement that sat at the front of the church. It contained the biggest roses she could find. A message in each program read that the arrangement represented all those who couldn't be present but were there in memory.

Amy was such a gorgeous young lady. She had just turned six. Her long red hair was pinned back, curls tumbling down her back. Her pink gown was patterned after Ann's own wedding dress. Ann had created this outfit to match her own. Amy held an arrangement of white and pink flowers, with more flowers and ribbon cascading down the front of her dress. She looked up at her father and grinned.

Ed winked back at Amy and then turned to concentrate on Ann. His eyes misted as he saw his blushing bride enter. In his eyes, she hadn't aged a day since the first time he watched her walk down the aisle. Her wedding dress flowed as she moved; it was like she was floating on air toward him. Time seemed to stand still.

Jake reached for Ed's hand and gently held Ed and Ann's hands together in his. Ann bent down so Jake could reach her and Jake kissed her cheek. Pastor Ron moved forward, so Jake's voice could be picked up in his microphone. "Who presents this beautiful bride today?"

Jake didn't need the microphone as he boomed, "My sister, Amy, and me are here to give Mom back to Dad." He had forgotten his lines, despite practising all yesterday and on the way to the church. The special mood Jake felt had flustered him. Everyone laughed and clapped. Jake thought he must have done OK, since no one seemed to correct him.

Holding hands, Ann and Ed turned to Pastor Ron. "It is not often I get to perform a wedding where the couple are renewing their vows after twenty-five years. I'm honoured to be here today to participate in this joyous celebration."

Just like the first wedding, Ann lost herself in Ed's deep blue eyes. She felt the love fold around her all over again. "Ann, Ed tells me he has his own vows. Are you ready to hear them and repeat your vows?" Pastor Ron interrupted her thoughts. She knew he had been speaking for some time, but she had to confess she never heard a word the pastor spoke until that minute.

"Ann, twenty-five years ago I stood before you with my knees trembling. I was full of love and adoration for you. But, I was scared to death that I'd never be able to meet your expectations of me and that somehow I would fail you. Today, I'm back here again, with my knees trembling just as much as before. I never thought I could be more in love with someone, but every day my love for you has grown deeper and stronger. I can remember some of the dumb things I have done and said, and I cannot promise that I will never do or say stupid things in the future. But today, in front of all our friends and families and our two children, I make this pledge to you. Ann, I love you with all my heart and soul. I will be by your side as long as the Lord permits. I will love you even after my last breath and promise to meet you on the other side when that time comes." As he spoke, tears formed in his eyes and by the time he finished, tiny droplets of moisture tumbled down his cheeks.

Ann felt her heart ready to burst wide open. She gazed into Ed's eyes, totally oblivious to anyone else in the room. Ed smiled down at her as she spoke. "Ed, you have made me speechless."

Amy fumbled to remove her shoe and presented Ann with a folded piece of paper. "Good thing I thought to bring your vows, Mom," she said as she handed her mother the paper with the notes that Ann had written down.

Ann took the paper, unfolded the page, and slowly refolded it. "Ed, you have given me love, laughter, joy, and tears. Like you, I had no idea I could feel more love for you every day. We have shared pain, happiness, and ecstasy. Our lives are full, and every moment of every day, I thank God for pointing me in the direction to find you. I promise to be with you as long as I live. I will be waiting on the other side for you. My love for you remains for all eternity."

"Ann and Ed, it gives me great joy to re-pronounce you husband and wife. Ed, you may kiss your lovely bride."

Bev, the church pianist, took her cue and started to play. Ed kissed Ann, and both of them reached out and pulled Jake and Amy into a group hug. Ann's beautiful bouquet of pink roses was crushed, but no one seemed to notice.

It was a great day. The sun shone as pictures were taken both inside and out. They went off to the small elementary school gym that they had set up and decorated the day before. Pink and white embellished the gym as they had the church. The smelly running shoe odour was replaced with the soft fragrance of flowers. Katherine had already brought over the arrangements from the church. She had incredible centerpieces on each table, flanked by small tea candles in crystal holders. The white tablecloths showed off the pink napkins. On each table, there was a picture of a popular couple, neatly framed in a simple silver frame. Guests wandered around, admiring the decorations and wondered about the pictures. The kitchen aromas of turkey and cabbage rolls drifted through the hallways. Ed and Ann hired the local caterer, but Ann had made the cabbage rolls and wedding cake herself.

Ed and Ann had invited all their family members and many friends. Some had been at their first wedding, while others were newer friends, made along their life journey. It was such fun to have a reason to get together. In all, there were just over one hundred fifty people at the gym.

The dinner was ready, and all the tables were full. Ed's brother, Owen, was master of ceremonies and called in everyone. Sara had set up the process to get everyone to the buffet tables. Each table had a famous couple, and Owen had made her a wheel with matching pictures attached. Sara would spun the wheel, and the couple on whom the wheel landed was the next table to head to the buffet table. Owen kept a running commentary sparkled with jokes about the famous couple and comparisons to Ed and Ann. When he chose Owen, Ed knew it would be like he and Ann were the guests of honour at a roast. But, unlike their first wedding, there was so little stress to this party. It was meant to be fun, and that was the main theme for the entire day. Also unlike their first wedding, they had specifically requested no gifts.

Owen and Sara put a lot of work into the dinner program. They organized skits and had several toasts and a whole lot of special words and stories from family and friends. Ann laughed until tears rolled down her cheeks.

As the dinner and speeches were rolling to a finish, several friends had got up and moved to the front. Ann wondered what was going to happen next. Bruce, Bert, and Al made a performance over who would get the microphone. Bruce won and began, "As you're aware, Ann and Ed asked us not to bring any gifts for them, but you're probably aware, I've never been one to follow orders."

Ann frowned; she didn't think she liked where this was going. Bruce stuck his tongue at both her and Ed and continued. "So, we snooped around to find out where these guys were going for their first and second honeymoon rolled into one. You may not know, but they skipped the first honeymoon in favour of a down payment on their house. But now the house is paid for, and Ed wanted to spare no expense for Ann, wanting to take her to Drumheller and to Dinosaur Park. Bert and Al and I talked him into something a little more special. Of course, we had our wives putting their two cents worth in when they heard about the plan."

Bert took the microphone out of Bruce's hand. "What Bruce is trying to say is that we helped make a better plan. And Ann, we know you're going to love us for this. It should probably be worth a lemon pie at least." Everyone understood Bert's heart was really a giant lemon pie. As Bert spoke, Al and Bruce pulled a big piece of cardboard from around the corner of the stage. It was all covered up, and everyone was curious.

"Can Ann and Ed come over here beside me, so we can get a better view of this handsome couple?" With that, Ann and Ed walked around the head table and over to the side to the microphone stand. Bert handed Ed the microphone and walked over to Al and Bruce. The DJ sitting on the stage sounded a lengthy drum roll. Together, they tore off the big bow and wrapping paper to reveal a giant picture of the Eiffel Tower. Next to the Eiffel Tower was a series of envelopes taped to the picture.

Ann gazed at the picture, and as the light bulb came on in her head, she turned to look up at Ed, who was grinning from ear to ear. He was nodding like a spring toy. Her eyes grew large, and she leaned into Ed. "Are you kidding? You arranged this without me knowing?"

"Well, you were a little busy with something about lists and a little get-together for our anniversary." Ed chuckled.

"It's my turn." Al grabbed the microphone from Ed. "You may have planned the trip, but we have a few changes we would like to present. Yep, first of all, the place you arranged to stay, not good enough for a woman who has put up with you for twenty-five years. We changed the reservation. You guys are now staying at a nineteenth-century luxury spa hotel." Al showed a picture of the hotel. He bowed to the crowd as they applauded.

It was now Bert's turn, and he took control of the microphone. "Second, you need to have a romantic dinner. We have been told the best place in Paris to eat is in the dining room right in the Eiffel Tower. We have booked you two seats, which includes the trip up the Eiffel Tower in a private elevator."

Bert handed the microphone to Bruce. "We also will be treating you to a fabulous tour of the Palace of Versailles, including a car and driver to transport you to the palace. Once you have finished your tour, you will go to the Le Gordon Ramsay au Trianon restaurant of the Hotel Trianon Palace Versailles Waldorf-Astoria Hotel, where you will eat in a stunning five-star facility that offers the most exquisite French fare. When you're full, the car and driver will deliver you back to your hotel in Paris, safe and sound." Bert was starting to sound more like Bob Parker from the *Price Is Right*.

Al took over and did his best impression of Richard Dawson from *Family Feud*. "There is one small glitch in your original plan, Ed: the travel dates. Because you wouldn't tell us and we couldn't find out exactly when you planned the trip, and because you have so many holidays scheduled this year, we took it upon ourselves to have tickets for you to fly out tomorrow evening. Everything has been arranged at work. Tickets are for a first-class trip with Air Canada."

At this point, people could no longer contain their excitement in the gift they had all pitched in to purchase for their favourite couple. Everyone cheered and clinked their spoons against their wineglasses.

Neither Ann or Ed were prepared for any of this, and the shocked and stunned faces they had were later displayed by Connie, who had taken a series of pictures during the entire presentation. Tears ran down Ann's face. Ed stood in total shock. Amy and Jake moved over to their parents and took their hands.

Not wanting to be left out, the DJ for the evening started to play the couple's first dance and asked everyone to join hands around the couple as they danced to Anne Murray's "You Needed Me." It had always been their song, and they would have forgotten the rest of the wedding guests had it not been that the entire hall was gathered around them.

Al moved in and passed Ed the microphone. Ed waited until the song was finished, and he gentled whispered in Ann's ear that he loved her.

In the middle of the dance floor, Ed started to speak; he had to wait several minutes until the noise settled so he could hear himself.

"Thank you so much, all of you." Ed struggled to keep his voice strong. Ann squeezed his hand as hard as she could. That did it, Ed continued. "Ann and I are unbelievably blessed with the family and friends we have. Each and every one of you has been with our little family through the ups and downs, and there are just no words I can think of that begin to feel adequate. But, from the bottom of our hearts, thank you." He looked down at Jake and Amy and across to Ann. They all held hands. "You have left all of us speechless."

At that point, Amy reached up and secured the microphone from her father's hand. "Now, let's eat Mommy's fancy wedding cake."

The mood was festive, and everyone joined on the dance floor. Amy got her wish, and once the next dance was finished, Ann and Ed cut the cake. Ann had made the cake with a little something special for each of her family: the first layer was chocolate with chocolate filling for Jake and Amy, the second layer was carrot cake with cream cheese filling for Ed, and the top was her favourite vanilla with white chocolate mousse filling. The cake was decorated with Ann's special touch. The first layer represented Jake and Amy, and Ann had put tiny pink ballet slippers and little blue dump trucks all moulded from coloured chocolate. The second layer was trimmed with tiny pink flowers and silver beads. On the top layer, Ann had found a tiny music box with a dancing bride and groom. She added a silver 25 behind it.

She planned to put this cake top inside her china cabinet, alongside the top from her first wedding.

Later, as the party was ending, Ann sat with her friends, Connie, Joyce, and Cheryl. They told her they'd arranged for Amy and Jake to stay with Owen and Sara while she and Ed were in Paris.

"I have so much to do. I'll never be ready. I have suitcases to pack, things to buy; my house is a mess with all the people and events of the past couple of days." Panic was starting to set in.

"The house is being cleaned as we speak," Joyce announced. "You think we'd leave our best friend in such a dilemma."

"The kids' clothes have been taken care of. In fact, their suitcases are already in Owen's car. You just have to pack for you and Ed, and we've already gone through your closet and selected stuff we think you'll need to pack. Anything else you can buy in Paris." Cheryl had spent time the day before packing the kids' stuff, while everyone else was at the gym decorating and setting up.

"Ed and I haven't been away from Jake or Amy since Amy was born. I'm not sure we can handle being away for a whole week." A new set of concerns hit Ann. "What if the kids need us, and we're halfway around the world."

Connie hugged her friend. "You and Ed need some time together, and this is why you have us for friends."

They all laughed and spent the next hour discussing what each of the women had learned about Paris.

The next day was a rush. Just as Joyce had promised, Ann arrived home later that night to a sparkling clean house. Getting up the next morning was amazing, since the chores and work Ann had anticipated she would have do was already completed. Everything on her list was finished hours before they left for the airport. She sat down with Ed, Jake, and Amy, and they discussed the upcoming week. Ann made notes for Sara on where and what each child had on their schedule. Amy was busy with swimming lessons, both kids had piano lessons, and Jake had a birthday party to attend. Ann was most concerned about how the children felt.

Her three friends arrived with breakfast muffins and hot coffee and set in to help organize both Ann and Ed to be ready for their trip to the airport. Ann already had most of the packing done. She'd followed Katherine's advice and put all the clothes she thought they should take on the bed. Then, she took away half of them. She hoped her sister knew what she was talking about. She knew if they were missing something that shopping for it in Paris would be a treat.

Owen and Sara arrive early, so they could have lunch and then head to the airport. Owen planned for the children to watch some airplanes fly out, and they were going to head to the air museum.

"You have a list of all the numbers where you can reach us. Right?"

"That's the third time you have asked me that today. If I didn't know better, I'd think you didn't trust my parenting skills." Owen winked at Ann, hoping to keep the conversation light. He knew Ann was very close to tears.

It was with trepidation that Ann and Ed got out of the car at the airport. Ann was the one who had never been away from the children for any length of time, and even though she looked forward to spending some romantic time with Ed, she was anxious about leaving.

Jake and Amy were really energized. They were looking forward to spending time with their uncle and aunt out at their acreage. As an only child, their son, Trevor, had grown up with the most envious collection of toys, and Jake especially looked forward to spending time entertaining himself with the treasures that were so bountiful. Amy, on the other hand, was looking forward to Aunty Sara letting her make cookies for Uncle Owen. Because he was getting old, it was decided that Finnegan would be better off staying in town with Joyce and Al. He enjoyed his short walks over to visit Joyce for tea and cake, so he didn't seem to take offence to missing out on a trip to the airport and then off to the acreage. He was past his squirrel chasing days. He would rather spend his days lounging in his bed, his favourite toys next to him, and getting the odd piece of cake that Joyce would give him.

They boarded the plane and found themselves seated in the comfortable La-Z-Boy–like leather seats in first class. Ed squeezed Ann's hand. "This is going to be the best honeymoon two people could every have."

Ann smiled back as the stewardess delivered them each a glass of champagne. She snuggled down against Ed and sipped her drink. Ed put his arm around her; this was going to be a wonderful time alone together. She had planned to send thank you notes to all their friends and family for such a special gift during the flight over, but maybe on the way home.

Chapter Twenty-One

"Hello, Mrs. Murray. My name is Emily, and I'm your nurse for the evening. Looks like you've been able to catch a little nap after your husband and son left."

Emily busies herself with checking Ann's incision. She also checks the computer for reports from all the equipment. She notes the same irregularities as previous staff and observes that the information continues to be transmitted to Dr. Murray and Dr. Morton.

Ann adjusts her bed so she's sitting up a bit more. "When am I going to be allowed to get out of bed?"

"Well that would be up to Dr. Murray. You might want to ask her next time she drops by. If you like, we can adjust the bed so you're more comfortable. Supper will be here in a couple of minutes, and liquids are definitely easier to eat when you're sitting up. Just let me know if it becomes uncomfortable."

Emily moves the bed until Ann is more comfortable. "I see I must have slept this afternoon. I missed my sister and sister-in-law." Ann sees cards sitting on her stand and recognizes the writing on each. Emily hands them to her, along with her reading glasses.

"Thanks. I have not put these on for a couple of days. I haven't been reading much." Ann opens the cards and reads the notes. "My sister and sister-in-law are a blast. Probably a good thing I was asleep. They can make me laugh until I cry. That wouldn't be good for this incision." Ann opens her gown and gazes at the sight. "Lying down, I haven't been able to get a real picture of what my chest looks like. Is this what heart surgery incisions always look like?"

"Oh, they vary depending on what we're doing, but this is pretty typical. With all the modern surgery inventions, the incision for these surgeries hasn't changed much. But yours is healing nicely. No sign of infection, no strain on the staples. All in all, I would classify you as a model patient. I wish all my patients were as good as you. No demands, easy to talk to; it's a pleasure to come into your room. You probably heard horror stories, since your daughter is the head doctor here."

"Actually, Amy never discusses work with me. When she comes to visit, we have so many things to talk about work never gets to the top. Her schedule's pretty full, so when we have time, we love to chat about music and friends and gardening."

Emily deposits Ann's supper tray on the stand. "Let's see what you're having for supper: soup, ice cream, juice, and you will be happy to know there is no JELL-O." Ann looks up. Emily's eyes twinkle. "It says you don't like food that moves."

They both chuckle as Ann picks up her spoon and taste her broth. "Not bad. I thought all hospital food was supposed to taste terrible. This is good."

"Must be the drugs affecting your taste buds," Emily asserts. "Most people complain, and I've seen lots of family and friends bring food. Paul's Drive Inn down the road was made popular, I think, by family and friends of patients here at the hospital."

Emily chats and keeps Ann company as she eats her meal. Ann's beginning to feel better and wishes she could get up and move around a bit. She remembers Ed telling her that he and Jake were going to meet Amy for an early supper. She knows they'll be back later.

Emily sees the small iPod that sits next to Ann's cards. "I see you have some music here. Would you like me to connect this up?" She didn't wait for an answer, and in just a couple of minutes, an old Elvis song fills the room, as Emily connected it into the room speaker. "Wow, what a great song. You must love oldies."

"Actually, they're not oldies to me; they're the songs I grew up with over the years. Jake bought me this for Christmas last year. He must have spent hours tracking down all my favourite songs and singers. It's entertained me on a regular basis."

Ann finishes up the food on her tray. "Wow, I didn't realize I was even hungry, but look at this, I managed to eat everything on my tray."

Emily checks the instruments again, puts on a soft light for Ann, and picks up the tray, "If you need me, just buzz. I'm close by."

Ann nods and lies back to listen to the music. The Beach Boys are singing their "California Girls" song.

Chapter Twenty-Two

The arena was full, and the noise was comparable to a rock concert. The crowd's going wild, with "We will, We will, rock you" booming through the speakers. It's the last game of the tournament. Jake's the captain of the Riverside peewee team. He'd turned twelve earlier in the year.

Jake had moved up the ranks, starting when he was five years old. He spent the first six months after Christmas, when he got his first pair of skates from his aunt and uncle, learning to skate. By the time he started hockey the following fall, he'd watched hockey along his big cousins and learned all their moves. He was small, but he could out skate all the players in the league. By the time he hit Atoms level, scouts from across Canada and the United States were watching him.

Ann told him the same thing her sister had told her sons: "Hockey is a game; you play it for fun. When it's not fun anymore, walk away." She said the same thing at the beginning of every season, and by the end of the season, she always heard the same thing, "its still fun."

Ann and Amy were on the edge of their seats in the Grande Prairie Canada Games Arena. This was the first time Riverside had made it all the way to the top of the league and qualified for a provincial tournament. It's pretty exciting. They'd travelled together on a chartered bus. Several parents joined them to fill up the bus. The rest of the parents organized a second bus. This was a big deal for the little hockey community, so the benches had its share of very loud and supportive family and fans.

"Come on, Jake, you can do it." As assistant coach, Ed had to try to contain himself, but with the score tied and three minutes into overtime, it was impossible. He let himself get into the moment, moved by the crowd. He couldn't help it; he was so proud of his son.

Ed realized he had to focus back on the game and saw the perfect play opportunity that he and Jake had discussed only last week with Alex. Alex shared it with them when he caught up to them at a hockey game in Airdrie. He's playing on the university hockey team while getting his engineering degree. Alex's university coach taught the moves to his team. Just the previous week, they'd used this play to win their last university game. Ed had shared this play with the coach on the way up to the provincial tournament in Grande Prairie. It had been a long bus trip, and they had lots of time to strategize on how to play, especially since they'd be playing with many teams who had been champions in their own leagues and were veterans of the provincial tournament. They knew the games would be tough to win.

"Coach, I think we should try those moves that Alex shared with us. Remember, it helped them win the university championship game last week."

"I like it," the coach told Ed and signalled Jake to call time-out. "I think you're right. This is the perfect time to try out those new moves."

As the team huddled around their coach, he gave his instructions. "Jake, we're putting Colton back; we need his muscle to get this next play to work. We need to have some strength to match the speed and keep these guys off guard. Justin, take a breather. Colton, hit the ice. Start with looky look and move into the back door. Jake, you handle the back door. Colton, you lead looky look. Let's do it."

The team broke and headed back to center ice. It was their last time-out, and with only seconds on the clock, they had to make every move count.

The puck dropped; there was total chaos in the stands. Jake and his team didn't seem to hear the roar of the crowd. They moved through their plays like pros. Suddenly, Jake broke away, and Colton passed the puck. Jake took his shot. It seemed to be moving toward the edge of the net. Suddenly, like magic, the puck hit the side of the net and bounced in. The crowd were on their feet and went wild.

Tears ran down Ann's face as she hugged Amy. Both were jumping up and down. Everyone in the stands rushed to hug Ann and Amy. All the parents, families, and friends were beside themselves with excitement.

The gloves and sticks were down, and the team surrounded Jake. Ed and Coach Adams skidded across the ice to their team. It was the tournament finale, and the team was now first-time provincial champions. Cameras were flashing around the arena. Even the local television station had its reporter interviewing Jake and his team mates.

Back at the house, Jake brought in his latest addition to the trophy cabinet. He held it with pride as Ann took pictures. She had filled the camera with shots at the rink. Ed's beaming with pride, and even Jake's little sister was proud of her big brother.

Later that evening, the phone rang. It was a scout who wanted to meet Ed and Ann the next morning. Rob McMillan had seen a lot of skill on the ice but nothing like this twelve-year-old, and he wanted him in his summer training camp. He'd told that to Ed on the phone.

Later that evening Ed discussed his conversation with Ann. "What are we going to do?"

"I think that is a decision Jake has to make. I know he likes to play hockey, but is it something he's willing to do all summer. Besides, if we say no, it could be something that all of us regret for the rest of our lives. Jake needs to make the decision. Let's wait to hear what this guy has to say before we do or say anything."

"I love it when you're right and we have an idea of how to handle this." Ed put his arms around Ann and kissed her. "It's getting late, and we've had a full day. Let's sleep on it."

Promptly at ten the next morning, the doorbell rang. Finnegan announced their visitor. "Answer the door, Jake. My hands are wet," hollered Ed. Jake answered the door and brought Rob into the kitchen, where his father was fixing the garbage disposal. It had plugged again. Ann was in the laundry room.

"Mom, Mr. McMillan's here to meet with us," Jake shouted down the stairs to the laundry room. By the time Ann made it up the stairs, Ed had poured three coffees. They were sitting around the kitchen island, waiting for her.

"At least offer the poor man a chair at the table if we are not going to the living room." Ann was shocked at her husband's poor manners.

"I asked to sit here, Mrs. Murray. I'm pleased to meet you." Rob stood as she entered the room and put his hand out to shake her hand.

"Nice to meet you, Mr. McMillan."

"Please call me Rob. I saw the game yesterday in Grande Prairie. In fact, I've seen several games over the past weeks. Jake, your name's moving around the hockey circles. Every scout who has seen you play is very impressed with what we've seen." Rob liked to get right to the point.

"Thank you, sir," Jake replied. He had heard so many adults comment about his game, he was no longer flattered or excited.

"We want you to come to our summer hockey camp in Vancouver for the months of July and August. I'm here offering you a chance to work on your skills with professional coaches. We have some of the best in Canada working with us in the summer months, along with several players."

Ed started to reply, but Ann took his hand. She wanted to hear Jake first. "Gee, sir, I'm not sure Mom and Dad can be away for that long. What would happen to Finnegan and Amy?" Jake looked first at his dad and then at his mom to see what they thought. "What do you guys think?"

"Jake, you know what I always tell you. Are you going to have fun?"

"Jake, I think you may have misunderstood. We're not interested in your parents. We want you to come to camp. Your parents wouldn't be included in our offer." Rob clarified his previous statement, as he immediately saw Jake had misunderstood the offer.

Jake looked at his dad and then at his mom. "But what about Disney World? This is the summer we are finally going to go."

"Jake," Ed spoke, "this is up to you, your decision. We'll respect whatever you decide. We can always do Disney World another time."

"Mr. McMillan, I really like to play hockey with my friends, but my family's been planning this trip all year. Besides, I don't want to be away from home for the summer holidays. That's the best time to be here."

Rob was shocked. He hadn't expected nor was prepared for this kind of response. Normally, the parents jumped at these kinds of offers. He looked at Ed and Ann to see what their response was. They appeared relieved. *No, that is impossible,* he thought.

"Sorry you had to make the trip here for nothing," Ed replied. "Ultimately the choice is Jake's."

Rob couldn't believe his ears. "Do you understand the potential in this offer? Starting at this level, by the time your son's finished high school, he could be ready to play in the farm leagues and have a real chance at playing professional hockey. Do you have any idea how much money the pros make?"

"Rob, I think you need to understand Jake plays hockey for the fun of the game. I'm not sure he's old enough to know what career he wants. Perhaps next year, when he's older, but right now, his father and I would never let him go to Vancouver alone for two months. He's only twelve years old." Ann needed Rob to appreciate their family situation.

"Thank you for the offer, Mr. McMillan." Jake put out his hand to shake Rob's. "I hope you have fun at camp. Like Mom said, maybe when I'm older, but right now I just want to have fun at Disney World. I have wanted to go there since I was little, and finally, this year we are going. My dad bought our tickets already."

"It was a real pleasure to meet you folks. Have a great summer." With that, Rob found his way to the door and let himself out.

Ann and Ed both beamed at Jake. They were so proud of the decisions he had made. They talked about the decision to make sure Jake really understood the choice he had just made.

Chapter Twenty-Three

Ann can feel someone in the room. She opens her eyes. Her iPod's still playing; Charlie Pride is belting out one of her favourites, "Kiss an Angel Good Morning."

Ed and Jake are just entering the room. "Hey my favourite men! I was pretty sure you'd be back."

Ed kisses her on the lips. "Kissing my angel good morning."

"Is it morning? Did I sleep right through the night?" Ann couldn't believe she could sleep so much.

"No, see, it's still light outside. It's only 7 o'clock in the evening. We have only be gone a couple of hours. I was just quoting Charles Pride." Ed winked at her with a big grin.

Jake is surprised his mother's looking so relaxed. She has some colour back in her face. "Hi, Mom. I brought you in a treat. Amy said you're allowed dairy products and I could bring you something liquid. I brought you a pineapple milkshake from Peters." He hands the shake to his mom. "Amy will be here later. She's got some kind of emergency down in ER."

Ann takes the milkshake and sucks on the straw. The cold shake feels so good running down her throat as she swallows. "This is great, thank you. I was thinking about asking for some ice cream. This is better than the vanilla ice cream I had at supper."

"Did you enjoy your supper?" Ann just nods. She is too busy enjoying her milkshake.

"We had a great supper, too. Katherine and Bill joined us, along with Owen and Sara. They had stopped here earlier, but you were asleep. The nurse told them where we were planning to eat. They didn't want to wake you up and will come back tomorrow to see you."

"The Keg, right?" Ann takes another gulp of her milkshake. She did not realize how much she was enjoying this milkshake. She usually stayed away from these high-calorie drinks, but not today.

"Aw, Mom, you know us way too well." Jake pulls up a chair and sits down.

"Owen and Sara brought us up to speed on the happenings in Arkansas. They just arrived back earlier today and came straight over to see you." Ed puts his hand on her forehead. "Sweetheart, you're looking good. You must have had a good rest."

"I do feel better actually. Emily, my nurse, put the iPod on. I lay back and listened to the music and must have dozed off. I was remembering the year the peewees took the league championship and Jake scored the winning goal."

Ann leans forward in earnest, "I was just thinking. Did we make a mistake; should we have let you go off to hockey camp that year?"

Jake slowly gets up, walks over to his mother, and bends over to look her in the eye. "Mom, I have never regretted a minute of my life with you and Dad. I made the decision. I had a lot of kids at school for quite a few days thinking I was the stupidest kid in the world to turn down that chance, but to me, it wasn't that important. It was definitely not as important as a trip with my family to Disney World. Do you know how badly I wanted to go to Disney World? First, it was wait until Amy was potty trained and then it was waiting until my arm healed after I broke it climbing Mr. Gillrie's apple tree. When Dad booked the tickets and brought them home, I'd decided right then and there that there was nothing, absolutely nothing that was going to keep me from being on that plane with you guys."

They spend the next hour reminiscing about their visit from Rob McMillan and their trip to Disney World. Jake reflects on his favourite rides and waiting had made the trip all the more fun for him.

Ann tries to hide a yawn, but Ed catches it. "You must be getting tired. We should call it a night and let you get some sleep."

"I just don't know why I should be tired. I have not even gotten out of bed, but for whatever reason, I feel exhausted." Ann openly yawns a second time.

"More tired than the time you spent the night at the hospital with me when I broke my arm again during the game with the meanest team in the league?" Jake gets a big grin from his mom. "Or more tired than the time just you and I took Colton and Justin with us to the tournament in Medicine Hat and shared the room with them?"

Ann's now grinning; she remembers how tired she'd been during both those events.

"Well there were certainly enough times over the years." Ed joins the game sharing their fun. "Did you know your mother never slept for almost a full week when you left home for university? We went through the same thing when your sister left. She walked around like a zombie for days."

"Ed, that's always been our little secret," Ann admonishes him. She's embarrassed to have this undisclosed information revealed to her son.

"Sorry, honey, but you did spend every night for a week going through all the photo albums and boxes of pictures. I was so worried about you and how long it would take for you to snap out of it." Ed teased her. "Jake, you missed the only chance to see the living room in total disaster and disarray. She had pictures and albums everywhere. It was a miracle when the Pioneer Girls leader broke her foot in three places and they needed someone to take her place. It got your mother out of the house and back to her old self." Ann sticks out her tongue out at Ed. He just laughs and reaches over to steal a kiss.

Jake relaxes for the first time in a couple of days. It's good to see his parents laughing and teasing each other again. He realizes how much fun they've made his life with their antics.

Ed checks his watch, "Seriously, we have to get out of here and let you get some sleep. Otherwise, you're going to be cranky tomorrow." Ed leans over. "I love you, sweetheart. Have a good night, and see you tomorrow." He kisses her again.

Jake hugs his mom. "Sweet dreams, Mom. See you in the morning."

Ann waves good-bye as Jake and Ed leave. She gazes out the window at the city skyline. With all the lights, Calgary never seems to get dark, and she can't see the stars like she can at home, when she looks out her bedroom window. Even with the streetlights of Riverside, she can see the stars. Of course, it's nothing like the sky at night, when they were out camping. Now those were stars. She drifts off.

Chapter Twenty-Four

Ann sat in the principal's office. Mr. Whiteside had called Ed and her to meet with him and Miss Fraser prior to parent–teacher interviews. It's Amy's first year of school.

"Amy's bored with her school curriculum. She's already reading at a third-grade level, and her math and science skills are well beyond that. We need to discuss options for her program," Mr. Whiteside said as Miss Fraser nodded in agreement.

"I try to keep her busy with more advanced work, but she's just not enjoying first grade. I'm worried about her. Jake could entertain himself with books and writing, but Amy wants more." Miss Fraser had been Jake's favourite teacher.

Ann and Ed had seen this coming and were equally as worried about Amy not being able to reach her full potential with the existing system in Riverside. They'd discussed this several times but really had no idea how to handle it. They'd met with Bill and Katherine one evening to discuss how they handled education with their oldest, Alex. He had a similar photographic memory. A grade-3 teacher recognized it, and they had transferred Alex to a private school located just a few blocks away from them. However, for Ed and Ann, that would mean Amy would have to endure a forty-five-minute ride every morning and evening.

"How would you handle this if she were your daughter?" Ed decided to ask Mr. Whiteside for his advice.

"There's a new program especially designed for gifted children at the Huntersville College. It only has twenty-five kids, and they're allowed to work at their own pace. They've hired three teachers who specialize in the field of eidetic memory."

Ed looked puzzled and was about to ask. Before he could, Mr. Whiteside continued. "It's the ability to look at a page in a book and then recall it word for word and retain the information for long periods of time. The experts believe that if a child with this amazing eidetic image ability doesn't have proper training, they'll gradually lose this ability in adolescence, as the mind learns to be more interested in what's happening in the world and they don't continue to take the time to practice and develop their abilities."

Miss Fraser took over. "While I was in university, a team of professors obtained funding to present special programs for children to improve and widen their skills. They also wanted to be able to increase the volume of information retained. I spoke with one of the professors, and he advised me they actually had a full curriculum developed and recently received government consent to set up a pilot. For some reason, Huntersville College was picked. I think it's because they had extra room in their new faculty wing, and they offered it to the professors. There is some controversy around this, but the professors have enough scientific research to support the program."

"Before we were to do something like this, we need to speak with Amy. Can we meet the teachers and visit the classroom in Huntersville." Ed didn't want to pressure his daughter.

"What about Jake? Is it possible to move both children in this program, if we like it?" Ann had also been concerned for Jake's education as well.

"Of course. We're here to help out any way we can. We want to do what's best for Amy and for Jake. They're both great students, and they're our priority in all this. I'd suggest that we set up a meeting once you've spoken to Amy and Jake. Then we can all visit the classroom. Miss Fraser and I are eager to see this program ourselves."

Ed noticed Miss Fraser was chewing on her lip. "Are you concerned about something, Miss Fraser?"

"I'm not sure how much this program costs. I know the province is paying for some of it as a special pilot project, and I know you'll be able to access the money the Department of Education pays the school board, but I don't want to get your hopes up and then find out it's beyond your financial reach."

"Is there any way, Mr. Whiteside, you could find out before we go forward? We do have money set aside for the children's education, but that was marked for university." Ed knew they had more than sufficient funds for the children's future. Jeff and Mary and their life insurance policies and inheritance had seen to that. They hadn't touched a dime of the money, and it was locked in at a very good interest rate. But moving forward without knowing the costs was just not something Ed did.

"Before we speak with either of the children, perhaps we should get some information and maybe have another meeting once we have the details. We're not even sure there'd be room in the program." Ed smiled at Ann; she was always the practical person. "I don't want to introduce a lot of possibilities to either Amy or Jake until we know this is something we can make happen."

"Can you call us when you get the information, and we'll come back to talk more about it. After that, we could set up an appointment to tour the program, all of us together." Ed rose, signalling the meeting was over.

Mr. Whiteside and Miss Fraser shook hands with Ann and Ed. "I'll try to get as much information as possible, and Miss Fraser can call you to set up a time for us to get back together. In the meantime, thank you for all the time you have volunteered to this school with both Jake and Amy. We appreciate parents like you very much."

Since Joyce was staying with Amy and Jake, Ed suggested they go for coffee to talk about the idea further before they went home. He knew Amy would want to know all about the meeting. Long gone were the days when they could spell out words, as both Jake and Amy could figure out the words way too fast. Now they either had to talk after the children were asleep or sneak out for a coffee someplace. When Ed did shift work, they often had time together during the day. But with his recent promotion—Ed now managed the plant—it meant he was there Monday to Friday, leaving them little extra time together.

True to her word, Miss Fraser called shortly after lunch the next day. She'd collected all the information and wondered if they could meet after school. Ann called the plant to see if Ed could manage another early day.

At 4:30 that afternoon, they were back in Mr. Whiteside's office. Miss Fraser had several sheets of paper ready for them. The costs were not quite as high as Ed and Ann had anticipated, but if she went back to the law office part time, they could swing it without withdrawing any funds from the education fund they had set up.

They hoped both children would be interested in participating in the program. Miss Fraser had made arrangements for them to meet at the college on Friday, since there was no school for the children that day. Ed and Ann would discuss this with the children, and they'd all go to the college to meet the teachers and learn about the program.

After supper that evening, they sat both Amy and Jake together to discuss this opportunity and get a feel for how the children would respond. To their surprise, their only concern was about their friends. Could they still spend time with their friends? Ed explained they could play together after school and on the weekends. He reminded them that most of their friends lived nearby, and although they couldn't walk back and forth to school, there would be lots of time for them to play together. Jake worried most about hockey practice. Ed told him the new school wouldn't interfere with his hockey. Amy wanted to learn more about what kinds of things they would be doing, things different from what Miss Fraser was doing in class.

"This is why Miss Fraser has arranged for all of us to meet with her at Huntersville College and tour the program. You can meet the teachers and ask them all the questions you can think of," Ed explained.

"You should make a list of questions you want to ask," Ann suggested. "I already have my list started, so we can compare notes and see what else we need to know."

They then spent time coming up with questions to ask on Friday's tour. Ann and Ed were pleased to hear the children so receptive to the possibility of changing schools. The chimes from the clock interrupted them, and Ann was surprised that an hour and half had gone by. Amy went off to find a book for the bedtime story before she headed for the bath tub. It was her night to choose the book. Jake headed for the shower.

"I'm not sure about parenting," confessed Ed. "Every time we expect these guys to ask a lot of questions and give us a hard time, they don't. And when I think things are going to be easy, it's not. How will we ever know what to expect?"

"I guess we just go with the flow. And right now, speaking of flow, I need to see if Amy is running the tub over and make sure Jake has the shower door shut. I'm not really ready for water issues tonight." Ann took off down the hall, first to Amy's room to check on Amy and the water in the tub in her bathroom and then to see about Jake in his bathroom.

Ann was glad they built their house with a bathroom in each of the four bedrooms. It was a little pricy at the time, but it had more than paid for itself. Ann remembered the arguments she and her sister had with only one bathroom in the house. This house had been built with the intention of filling each room with children. Now, she saw it was well worth the extra money. It was hectic if the bathrooms all need to be cleaned, but for getting the kids ready for bed, it was great—especially now, as Amy was old enough to not want her dad or brother around when she was in the tub. She still loved putting her dolls in the tub with her and playing with them.

Friday morning found Jake and Amy with Ann and Ed at the Huntersville College. Miss Fraser and Mr. Whiteside were waiting outside the building as planned. "Glad to see you again." Mr. Whiteside shook hands with all four of them. "Mr. Hatfield will meet us in just a few minutes. He is the principal and in charge of the program. He also teaches social and history." Mr. Whiteside led the group as they went down the hallway toward the classrooms. "Mr. Hatfield will show you the classrooms and introduce you to the other two teachers."

"How many students are in the program?" Ed was looking at all the doors as they walked through the maze of hallways and doors.

"Right now, they have twenty-five students, but they can handle three more before the program is officially full." Miss Fraser was following with the children.

"How old is everyone?" Jake was curious.

"They vary in age from six to twelve years old. There are twelve boys and thirteen girls," answered Miss Fraser. "They come from as far south in Alberta as Lethbridge and north into the territories. They have a student from Switzerland, two from Toronto, one from Mexico, and two from Jordan."

By this time, they had reached the classroom with Mr. Hatfield's name on the door. Mr. Whiteside knocked and opened the door. Several students were sitting in front of their own computer. Since there were only had ten computers in their entire elementary school, he was already impressed. The students looked up as they entered, and Mr. Hatfield approached from the back of the room.

"Welcome to my classroom. You must be Mr. Whiteside." He extended his hand.

"Thank you for taking time to meet with us. I'm Herb Whiteside." He shook hands.

"I would like to introduce you to Miss Fraser, one of my grade-1 teachers, Mr and Mrs. Murray, and, of course, this is Jake and this is Amy."

Both children shook hands with Mr. Hatfield. "Let me introduce you to my students." He led Jake and Amy, with the adults following behind. "This is Christopher, Noah, Ethan, Owen, Sophie, Ava, Isabella, and Emily. We are studying history right now."

The students politely shook hands with each other and the adults. Then, they returned to their computers and their studies.

Mr. Hatfield escorted the group to the next classroom. As they walked down the hall, he suggested they meet in his office after the tour to discuss the curriculum, how the program functioned, and the objectives for each student.

The classroom across from Mr. Hatfield's belonged to Mr. Anderson. Mr. Hatfield knocked on the door but didn't wait for an answer. "Hello, Mr. Anderson. May I interrupt for a couple minutes? There are some folks I would you to meet." The students again were all working on their own computers. Now even Ed was impressed. They had a control room full of computers at the plant, but Pegasus could afford it. This was a pilot project and a school.

Mr. Hatfield introduced Amy and Jake and the adults, just as he had done to his class. He knew all the students by name. "Mr. Anderson is in charge of the science programs, which include biology, chemistry, physics, and mathematics." Mr. Hatfield motioned to Mr. Anderson, who went to his computer at the front of the room.

"As you can see, we have a lot of really special equipment." He directed their attention to the whiteboard at the front of the room. "This is an invention we are testing for some friends. Right now we call it our smart board."

As he spoke, Mr. Anderson was typing on his computer, and the information was displaced on the whiteboard. Jake and Amy stared, as did Mr. Whiteside and Miss Fraser. He demonstrated a number of different functions. The board was divided into four sections: math, chemistry, physics, and biology. He walked over to the board, and with a touch of his finger to the board, he flipped the page of the math book as it was displayed, bringing up a formula from the new page. It filled the section of the board dedicated to math. He then asked Joshua to complete the formula. As Joshua typed on his computer, the formula was completed and the answer appeared.

"The board's had a few improvements that we worked on directly with the inventors. It works well for us, since each teacher teaches multiple subjects. Each student works at his or her own pace, so there could be several levels of work being done at the same time. Or, we can work together on one project." Mr. Anderson flipped the computer to a new page that filled the entire board.

By now, all four adults stood with their mouths open. Not one had seen anything like this.

"This is just one of the neat pieces of equipment we get to play with." Mr. Hatfield got their focus back on him. "We have many friends in the technology industry who like to work with our group. They provide the equipment, and we help them fine-tune it. It helps support our project."

"Thank you, Mr. Anderson. I will let you get back to your class. Good-bye students," said Mr. Hatfield.

Good-byes from the students and Mr. Anderson were received with a thank you from each of Mr. Whiteside's little group.

"Next, we'll go to Miss Brooke's classroom." They walked a short distance to the end of the hall. "Miss Brooke teaches English, literature, French, Spanish, and music." Again, Mr. Hatfield knocked at the door and entered. Miss Brooke's classroom was enormous compared to the previous two rooms and appeared to be divided into several sections. The front sections were exactly the same as the others, with two rows of students, each desk with its own computer. Jake looked to the front: sure enough, another smart board.

Miss Brooke was rushing from the very back, "I'm so sorry, Mr. Hatfield. It is music class, and we are in the music room. Please come and join us."

Mr. Hatfield introduced Jake and Amy and the adults to Miss Brooke. "Come," she said, "I have a chance to show off my students, and you can critique our little program. I hope you will enjoy this. We are practising for the college alumni evening. We are the entertainment for the function."

They followed her back to her music room. There was an array of chairs with students and instruments in a semi-circle. They looked up and smiled. As before, Mr. Hatfield introduced the students, each giving a wave. Miss Brooke moved in front and picked up her baton. When she raised it, the students picked up their instruments and began to play. Mr. Hatfield motioned for his group to sit on the chairs lined up in front of Miss Brooke, against the back wall. They sat in amazement. It was a small symphony orchestra. The students played five pieces, ranging from a piece from "Phantom of the Opera," to a jazz song, to a marching band–type song, and finishing with a collection of music from Elvis Presley. When the group concluded, the visitors jumped up and clapped. The band and Miss Brooke bowed low. The clapping continued, as their small audience truly enjoyed this live entertainment.

Miss Brooke looked at her watch: it was noon. "Class, its lunchtime. Go ahead and break for your lunch. I think we're good until tomorrow. We can have a dress rehearsal in the morning in the main hall while the tables are being set up."

"I apologize if I messed up your schedule, Mr. Hatfield." Miss Brooke was concerned that she may have imposed on her boss and his guests.

"Not at all. We truly enjoyed your performance," Mr. Whiteside jumped in. "It was a pleasure to hear such a talented group of children at such young ages."

"Most students with eidetic memories love the challenge of learning to play musical instruments. Several of our students have a natural talent for music, and with the right encouragement, they can learn to play instruments very quickly. We have only been playing since September, since music is new to our program. I'm working with a group to develop a teaching program for much younger children just learning the alphabet. In return, they helped fund the instruments for my class."

"Does everyone get to choose their own instrument?" Amy had a love for music, and she and Jake were already taking piano lessons. The thought of playing something besides the piano sounded like fun.

"Well, my plan is that by the end of next year, all of the children can play each and every instrument we have available to us," replied Miss Brooke.

"Wow that sounds like fun." Amy grinned from ear to ear. "I'd love to be able to play the drums and trumpet."

"Let's not get ahead of ourselves," warned Ann. She needed a lot more information, and they had no idea if both children would even be accepted in the program.

"We can talk more in my office. I took the liberty of ordering in sandwiches for lunch. I hope that works with your schedule."

Mr. Whiteside looked at Ann, Ed, and Miss Fraser. They all eagerly nodded. "Seems we have unanimous support for that." Amy and Jake announced they were hungry, and a sandwich would be super.

They turned around and followed Mr. Hatfield back up the hallway to the first door on this wing. They had missed that door completely. It was labelled Principal, Eidetic Pilot.

Mr. Hatfield opened the door wide and waved his hand for his group to enter. Mr. Anderson was already in the room. "This lunch was quite a temptation for me. I thought you would never get here."

"We have guests," Mr. Hatfield responded with a hardy laugh. As you can see, we are pretty informal here. Please, let's sit down at the table here and have something to eat and drink as we discuss our little school. We call ourselves the Booster Mind Team."

Everyone gathered around the large table that had been set for lunch with trays of sandwiches, fruit, vegetables, and dessert squares of brownies, lemon bars and namimos. Three glass carafes were full of water and ice. There was a large variety of juices and pops in a big silver bowl piled with ice. Napkins and paper plates sat neatly to one side.

"Please help yourself. We can talk about our program and processes while we eat, and please feel free to interrupt with questions," suggested Mr. Hatfield as he reaches for another sandwich

Mr. Whiteside started by asking if Mr. Hatfield had received the package he had couriered over the day before. "Yes I did, and I must tell you I was very impressed in your presentation and information. All three of us have spent time looking at the data and we agree we see very compelling evidence of eidetic memory. We'll want to do some additional testing just to be sure." Mr. Hatfield spoke as he filled his plate.

Ann helped Jake and Amy each choose a sandwich and added pickles and cheese, along with pieces of celery, broccoli, and carrots. With a good variety of food on each place, she opened two small apple juices and passed them to the children.

"Can you tell us how your program works?" Ed, like Mr. Anderson, had already finished a sandwich and was adding another to his plate.

"I think I'll start with my classes and then ask Miss Brooke and Mr. Anderson to explain how their classes work. Each of us has developed our own training techniques and curriculum based on the Board of Education and major university entrance requirements for students planning to enter major fields such as medicine, engineering, law, and teaching. Our goal is to complete the entire primary education programs for each student in the next four years. Right now, we have funding for three years, but with the outreach we've been able to accomplish in the first year, I believe we'll have financial support up to the end of the fourth year, with commitments to expand after that."

Mr. Hatfield went on to explain his subjects and how each student worked at his or her specific pace. Once he was finished, Mr. Anderson took over to explain how the math and sciences were developed and what was entailed in his classes.

Miss Brooke began to give details of her core subjects and the addition of music. When she was finished, she noticed everyone had finished eating. "Perhaps you wouldn't mind if I took Amy and Jake back to my classroom. My class will be starting in just a few minutes, and I would love to bring the children back to my class while you continue your discussions."

Ann and Ed both nodded. The presentation was complete, and they needed specific facts to find out if the program was feasible for Jake and Amy. Mr. Anderson also excused himself.

Once the children left the room, Mr. Hatfield went straight to the facts. First, he explained that his students would be joining Miss Brooke for the first afternoon class while he continued his meeting. He'd planned this meeting very thoroughly, proving this was something he and the other teachers had done many times.

Jake and Amy would be able to participate in his program if the tests provided positive responses. And based on the tests Mr. Whiteside had already conducted, it appeared there would not be a problem. Both children showed strong abilities that would suggest they could move forward by several grades each year.

"If Jake and Amy finish that quickly, what happens next? I thought the entrance age for university was eighteen years." Ann was starting to grow concerned about how they'd cope. She remembered university and shuddered to think about her children leaving the protection of their home and school. She'd cried her heart out when Jake left for grade 1 and then again when Amy started school. She hadn't really thought how she'd handle them moving out of the house and having their own lives. She suddenly went into panic mode.

"There is no reason for concern. We have strong relationships with several universities, and they'll work together with us to allow courses to be taught by our staff here until the children are secure enough to move into that environment. Just because they finished their high school classes doesn't mean they'd leave the community. We have several retired university professors in the area who are prepared to work with all of the children who complete our program." Mr. Hatfield paused and took a sip of water.

"I must agree, I know many educators who have retired and moved into the region. They often contact me to see if there's anything they can assist with. It's most helpful to our school and our school board," Mr. Whiteside commented. He could see Ed watching Ann and felt her alarm and apprehension.

"I know Jake's teachers, and I've spoken often about what we can do to keep both of them interested in school. We can see they're bored, and it's difficult for them, the other children, and ourselves. We've all worked after school to try to design activities and special projects to keep them focussed. Amy's really showing signs of boredom," Miss Fraser commented. "Our concern is that they'll become disruptive if we can't keep them busy."

"Well, to be honest, Amy came home her first day of school and announced her class was full of babies who cried. I just assumed it was because of the emotions of first day and separation anxiety. It never occurred to me it was because she was bored." Miss Fraser's comments had started to bring new awareness to Ann about numerous comments the children had made over the past several weeks. She realized even Jake had expressed frustration that she hadn't picked up on until this moment.

"I'm beginning to realize we almost don't have a choice if we want to ensure our children stay active and grow in their learning abilities." Ed had been sitting back, listening, and he, too, realized what Ann had. Their kids were bored out of their minds and would very soon start to hate going to school. They couldn't let that happen.

"If we agree to this, how much will it cost to put both children into your school program?" Ann had seen all the equipment in each classroom and was now concerned about the costs. She knew there was plenty of money for their education but she didn't want to spend it all now and have nothing for university.

When Mr. Hatfield answered the question, both Ann and Ed couldn't hide their shock. "Is that for each child per year?" Ed gasped.

"Of course not. It's for the entire four-year program for both children." Mr. Hatfield grinned. He knew he shouldn't keep doing this to parents, but it was just something he did to make sure they were paying attention.

"The government will provide a portion of the funds, as they provide to the school board. So, that takes a chunk of the dollar number. It changes each year, but the difference is calculated at the midpoint of the school year, and an adjustment can be made at that time. The balance can be paid over the course of all four years, in monthly or quarterly payments. We've had a couple of parents who could afford the whole amount in one cheque, but that was pretty special. Most parents make monthly payments, and we're fine with that."

Ann and Ed were almost giddy. The amount Mr. Hatfield quoted was well within their price. They knew that it wouldn't be a big hardship.

"So, do you need some time to think about it and get back to me?" Mr. Hatfield needed to get back to his class.

"Well, I think we can say we want to move forward." Ed looked over at Ann as he spoke, and she nodded. "Of course, we'd like to speak with both Jake and Amy to be sure, but I watched both of them today, and I can see they're interested in being here."

"No problem. Why don't you take the weekend? I have some papers for you to review and fill out. Everything is explained in there. Bring them back on Monday morning, and we can start the process."

Everyone shook hands and left the room. They collected Jake and Amy from Miss Brooke's classroom. Both of them were excited about what they'd seen and heard. As they walked out to their vehicles, Mr. Whiteside suggested perhaps they'd like to meet with him after school on Monday to discuss the transition. They agreed and said their good-byes.

By the end of the month, both children were enrolled and members of the Booster Mind Team, as the students called themselves. In the morning, before work, Ann drove them to school. In the afternoon, she picked up the children. She soon met other parents dropping off their children. She discovered there were three other children who came from Riverside, and it wasn't long after that she organized a carpool. Not having to drive every day made things easier.

It was great to be back at the law office, working with James and Jean Stewart. Ann quickly realised she had missed working with these great lawyers. The practice had grown, and they now had three full-time staff. Ann worked three days a week, and that was enough. She still needed to make sure she had time for Amy and Jake and their after-school activities. However, she found they didn't need nearly as many activities as before. The new school program made both children look forward to going to classes. Each of them had formed their routine and found plenty of time to play with their friends after school and on the weekends. Even Finnegan eventually settled down; he was getting older, and changes in routine upset him. He adjusted to having the house to himself three days a week and seemed to know the children were happier with their new school arrangements.

Ann sometimes volunteered at their school and enjoyed meeting the other parents. The school had many social functions for the parents. It was a small group, and they all enjoyed meeting and working together.

Chapter Twenty-Five

It's almost 9 at night when Amy finally takes a break and decides to pop down to see her mother for a few minutes. In the elevator she takes out her phone to check messages. She sees she's received a call from Dr. Morton. He has followed up with a text message to schedule a time to speak to her in the morning. She quickly responds that she will be available. She'd have checked her messages before going into surgery, but every minute counts when a patient's suffering with severe heart problems. She knows Dr. Morton understands.

Amy checks with her mother's nurse at the ICU station. Emily's just been into Ann's room and woke her to have a snack. Ann's still awake. Emily smiles and tells Amy she thinks she's very lucky to have such a great mom, and she's available for adoption. Amy laughs as she pauses before she goes into her mother's room. She doesn't need to check the computer reports in her mother's room, since she'd just reviewed them in her office a short time ago.

She quietly slides open the glass door. She's sure her mom's asleep. Much to her surprise, Amy sees her mom, sitting up listening to her iPod. "I think you must be addicted to that iPod, Mom." She walks over and kisses her mom. "I thought you might be asleep. You were last night when I stopped to check up on you."

"Really, you stopped last night? Why didn't you wake me up? I've missed you. I kind of thought you'd be a regular here in my room." Ann speaks with a grin, and Amy's glad to see her mother's sense of humour coming back.

"I pop in on all my patients at irregular hours; it keeps everyone on their toes," Amy joked.

"So, come sit down, and tell me about what you're so worried about. I know something's on your mind. Now spill it. You know you can't keep secrets from me."

"Oh, I can think of a few things I've kept from you." Amy was confident about that.

"Don't try to change the subject. What's on those machines over there that you and all your staff look at?"

"Well, to be honest—"

"That's what I want," Ann interrupted.

"You understand these machines track everything that's happening in your body. This one here, for example, keeps track of how your body responds to your medications. This big boy keeps track of your heart, your blood pressure, your body temperature; pretty much when you move, this machine tells us. It lets the staff know if you're in pain."

Ann looked puzzled. "How can it know if I hurt?"

"Normally, when a patient is in pain, they start to move around, trying to find a position that hurts less. The machine monitors the movements and signals when you need more or stronger medication."

"So, I can't keep anything from you guys as long as I'm attached to that machine, right?"

"Exactly."

"So tell me, what kind of tales is this machine telling you about me." Ann's curious.

Amy smiles. "Right now, I know you have no pain, so you must have had your meds. Of course, I already know that since I spoke with Emily. By the way, she's available if you want to adopt another daughter."

Ann laughed. "I already have my favourite daughter, and while I'd love to have a favourite daughter-in-law, I'm too old to go through the stress of having another daughter leave home."

Amy smiled and went on. "Your blood pressure and heart rate are regular. You've always had low blood pressure, so for you, this is almost normal, just a little low for my liking, but we can work on that. Your heart rate's strong right now. The problem is that every once in a while, your heart rate seems to lose control of itself. It lasts a very short time, really just a couple of beats, but for my satisfaction, I need to have some more tests done. I've sent the information to Dr. Morgan. You remember him, right? Anyway, I'll talk with him in the morning and decide what steps to take next."

"Yes, I do remember. If he wasn't so much older than you and already married, I would've loved him as my son-in-law."

"Mom, quit trying to marry me off, especially to my friends."

"Amy, a good relationship starts out as a friendship. Your father and I have been best friends for over half a decade. That's how you start out."

"I know, Mom. You've mentioned that a time or several hundred before. Now, let's just talk. What were you thinking about when I came in? You looked a million miles away."

"Well, I woke up remembering your first days as a Booster Mind Team member. I was thinking about your teachers and how we ended up getting you and Jake into that program."

"I still remember. I was so bored in grade 1 with Miss Fraser. She's a nice teacher, but the others in the class were so slow at learning. When I met Mr. Anderson and Miss Brooke, learning came alive for me. I loved every minute. I remember when Mr. Anderson started letting me help him in the lab. The little lab kit I got for Christmas that year was so simple, but it was like a whole new world opened up."

"Yes, you used to come bouncing in the house after school. Jake was never as excited about the sciences as you were. He loved English and social studies. For a long time, I thought he'd end up as a teacher."

"Do you remember Victoria? I think she had an influence on Jake's decision to become a lawyer. He went to Yale the same year she went and then she went back home. I spent some time out there with them as well. I think for a while Jake thought she might be the one. But, I guess that one didn't work. It was my time with Victoria and her brother, Christopher that made me decide Yale was where I should go. I was pretty sure I knew medicine was for me, but for a while, I looked at research. We spent a lot of time researching new technology and equipment with Mr. Anderson, and I loved it so much. Good thing I was so lonesome for you and Dad and transferred back to University of Edmonton."

"Yale was so far away. I was thrilled when you called and told us you were coming back to take your final education back here. I know there were other influences that made that choice easier for you, but I figure someday, when you're ready, you'll tell me. You know, I'll be around for you."

Ann still remembers the pain she saw in Amy's eyes, but Amy refused to discuss it. To this day, Amy changes the subject whenever anyone mentioned her decision to move back to Alberta. Ann's always respected her children's privacy and knows they'll talk when they're ready. Ann and Ed have always encouraged their children to make decisions starting at an early age. It prepared them for the future and the avalanche of decisions they'll be forced to make. Once they left home, she knew they were adults and would make adult decisions. If they needed help, she and Ed were there for them.

"It was a good decision, and once I made it, I just knew in my heart that it was what I was meant to do. Lucky for me, I got to meet and learn under Dr. Morgan. He taught me so much about the quality of life. I fit into his team, and the experience made the decision to take this job easier—although I still question my decision to take on such a big responsibility. I'm never 100 percent sure I'm making the best decisions."

"Amy, you have to remember you're not the one who decides whether it's someone's time and whether that person lives or dies. God gave you your skills, but He still has the final say. No matter how hard you try, you can't allow yourself to second-guess what you feel is the right thing to do for your patients and even in your own life. You have to decide with your head and with your heart open to what God tells you."

"Mom, I love you so much. You're so wise. I'm so lucky to have you and Dad as my parents." Amy gives her mom such a big hug that Ann feels her heart pumping.

"Amy, you have to promise me that when I die, you're going to celebrate my life and not try to second-guess what you could've or should've done."

"Mom, I want God to let you live forever and never leave me."

"Amy, I will die, just as you will die. Just as your father will die. You know that. You also know you don't make that decision, and as much as you like to think you are, you're not in control. As for leaving you, I will always be with you. When you feel a breeze across your face, that's me kissing you. When you go to bed at night, I'll still tuck you in. I'll figure out a way to let you know that I'm with you. You will feel me in your heart and hear me whisper in your ear. Keep your heart open, and forget what your mind may tell you. I will always be with you."

Amy is saved from going completely to tears when Emily pops open the door and brings in a pot of tea. "I know, Dr. Murray, that you love your tea. I'm pretty sure your mom taught you about tea. I made you two a pot so you could have some tea. I hope it is OK. I brought some shortbread cookies my grandma made me. They melt in your mouth."

"Thanks, Emily. Actually, I've taken our patient off liquids, and she'll be on a soft diet starting right now with your cookies. Also, in the morning,

Maureen can take out the catheter, and Mom can get up and start moving around a bit. She still needs her intravenous for her meds, but we can start weaning her down."

"Does that mean I'm going to be able to go home soon?" Ann likes what she heard Amy tell Emily.

"Let's not rush, but if you behave yourself, I think that could happen in a few more days. I still have to run a few more tests and talk with Dr. Morgan. If your heart continues to perform properly, you can go home and continue with your plans for your fiftieth wedding anniversary."

"You and Mr. Murray have been married for half a century? That's amazing. I'm not sure I've met anyone who's made that record." Emily talks as she pours a cup of tea for Ann.

"Would you like to join us?" Ann invites.

"I wish I could. I have another patient to check on while his nurse is taking her dinner break, but I'll come back, and if you're still awake, I'll spend my break with you." Emily leaves Ann and Amy to their tea.

"She's such a nice lady." Ann munches on her shortbread cookie.

"You're right. She's one of my favourites."

For the next few minutes, they talk about Amy decorating her new house. She'd wanted to buy something closer to the hospital, and she found a perfect place just twenty minutes away. She just moved into it earlier in the month and hadn't had time to turn it into her home. In fact, she barely has any boxes unpacked.

After some discussion, Ann suggests Cheryl might be interested in taking on the challenge of working with Amy to get her house presentable. Over the course of their friendship, Ann's seen several amazing rooms on which Cheryl has worked. She's sure Cheryl would be thrilled to work on a whole house. With Amy so busy, she hopes Cheryl will want to tackle an entire house. She usually only does a room or two for a client. Ann hopes to feel well enough to add her two cents.

After they finish their tea and cookies, Amy starts to look a little withered. Ann suggests it is time for bed for both of them. Amy agrees, hugs her mom, and goes home for a few hours of sleep.

Chapter Twenty-Six

Amy feels the cool night breeze as she leaves the hospital. She can smell the flowers in the air. She walks to her small car in the parking lot. The lot is well lit, so staff always feels comfortable walking to their vehicles. There are also security cameras inside that monitor the entire complex, inside and out.

Amy opens the window so she can continue to enjoy the night air. Smiling, she reviews her conversations with her mom as she backs out of the lot.

She's nearly home when Amy feels the urge to turn around and head back to the hospital. She checks for traffic, spins around in the middle of the road, and guns her little car. A siren sounds behind her. "Darn," Amy mutters under her breath. A police cruiser, how'd she miss that? Amy pulls over and rolls down her window.

Andy's just finished spending the evening with his parents. He's on his way home when he notices this crazy driver. He hops out of his car, ready to give this driver several tickets, including dangerous driving. *What kind of idiot drives like this? Probably some drunk driver*, he thinks.

"Sorry, Officer. I'm a doctor, and I need to get back to the hospital." Amy's already pulled out her driver's license and registration, along with her pink card. She also has her hospital ID.

The officer checks her papers and hands them back. "Just be careful," he warns her. He notices her beautiful smile and big blue eyes. *What a beautiful woman*, he thinks.

"Thank you, sir." Amy smiles as she put away the papers and starts off again to the hospital.

Amy parks back at the lot and is just getting out of her car when her pager goes off. It's the ICU. She has problems. It's a 911 page, the highest level. Amy grabs her bag and scurries off to the entrance.

There's major action in the ICU; her patient from earlier is in deep trouble. Her team has already been called in. He was in such poor physical health when he arrived at the hospital earlier that evening. She was concerned he'd develop fluid on the lungs, a major concern and she'd alerted her staff to the possibility. Unfortunately, she's right in her diagnosis.

For the next two hours, Amy and her team work on this patient. Every time they think he's stable, his heart stops. They can't control the fluid as it forms on his lungs and around his heart. After a while, they can do no more, and they lose him. Amy's exhausted and frustrated. As usual, she blames herself. Then she remembers her earlier conversation with her mother. She takes a deep breath and gathers her staff. "We did everything right. You guys are an amazing team. It's late; let's call it a night. We can debrief in the morning."

She dismisses her team and goes to the doctor's lounge. She needs to shower and change out of scrubs before she can go anywhere. Amy's drained both physically and emotionally. She doesn't have the energy to attempt to drive home. Instead, she decides to sleep on the couch in her office.

On the way from the lounge to her office, she finds herself in front of her mother's room. She remembers the lounge chair she had put in the room so her dad could stay with her mother that first night. Quietly she slides the door open, closes it, and heads for the lounge chair. There's a blanket and pillow placed neatly at the bottom. She slips off her shoes and lies down. It's not as comfortable as her king-sized bed at home, but she's so tired she doesn't care. She's asleep when her head hits the pillow.

Ann wakes in the wee hours of the morning. While it's still dark, the full moon shines brightly in her room, and she sees someone sleeping in the lounge chair. She leans forward and recognizes Amy's red hair. She smiles and lies back. Amy must have been called back to the hospital.

Raising her bed so she can watch Amy sleep, she wishes Amy could see her own beauty. With big blue eyes and perfect ivory features, Amy could've been a model. Even in her teens, she was so busy looking into her microscopes she never took time to see herself as a beautiful women. Her hair's her most striking feature. It's a deep shade of strawberry blond, more strawberry than blond. Amy describes hair as her carrot mop, probably because of so many similar comparisons to carrots made over the years by her classmates.

Remembering the time Amy dyed it black brings a chuckle to Ann. She looked terrible. It took a trip to the hairdresser to get her colour back. After that, Amy never bothers with trying to change her hair. She usually has it in a ponytail and only remembers to cut it when she comes home and Ann drags her off to Lisa, her stylist.

She continues to watch Amy sleep and finds herself drifting into a deep sleep, the first sleep with no flashbacks.

Chapter Twenty-Seven

Jake stands at the door and watches in amazement. Both his mother and sister are sleeping. Amy's curled up on the chair, and his mother's cuddling her blankets.

Maureen approaches him and whispers, "We let them both sleep. They look so peaceful. Dr. Murray had a rough night. She was here most of the night, and she lost a patient. Your mother had her first night sleep with no pain meds."

"Mom had a good night?"

"She sure did. Her monitor suggests she didn't move all night."

Jake panicked. "Are you sure she's still alive?"

"Absolutely."

"She's progressing rather nicely. She's on soft foods as of today, and later this morning, we'll get her up."

Hearing voices, Amy opens her eyes to see Jake standing by the door. Jake sees Amy's now awake. "Good morning, sleepyhead. Did you get any rest in that chair?"

Realizing Amy's awake and hearing Jake's voice, Ann raises her bed so she can see her whole room. "Good morning, Jake. When did you get here?"

Jake moves into the room. He holds out a small book. Small being the appropriate word, since the book was only about three inches wide and four inches tall. "I thought you might want to read a little," he says as he greets his mother with a kiss on the cheek. "I thought it would be perfect for you. You can just slip it into your pocket."

Ann holds out her hand to take the book. She reads the title aloud. "*Words on Strength and Perseverance.* Such a small book with such a powerful title. Thank you. This is just the right size. I tried to hold my book your father brought in, but I couldn't hold it up to read it. This is perfect."

Amy looks at her watch. "Oh my gosh, I'm late for rounds. I have to get to my office and change."

Jumping up, Amy quickly looks for her shoes. "Thanks for the bed last night, Mom. I was way too tired to drive home. Glad you're here to visit Mom, Jake. Sorry I have to run. Love you both." Amy quickly tosses aside the blanket and dashes to the door. "See you later," comes from down the hall as Amy hurries to her office. She has a call with Dr. Morgan in just minutes, and she needs to get her paperwork ready for their review.

Noticing Dr. Murray fly past her desk, Maureen comes in to get Ann ready for the day. "Do you mind excusing us for just a few minutes?" Maureen asks Jake.

"No problem. Mom, I'll go down to grab a cup of coffee. Would you like a tea or something?"

"That would be nice."

"Great, I will be back in ten or so minutes."

As Jake leaves the room, Maureen gathers her instrument tray. "You get to lose the tubes today. No more catheters and only one small intravenous tube for your meds. We're going to try and get you into the shower a little later this morning, if you feel up to it. We need to get you up and moving around."

"You can't imagine how much I'm looking forward to a shower. Can I put on my own pyjamas and housecoat as well? I'm pretty sure I'm having family drop by, so it'd be nice to look presentable."

Ann chats as Maureen carries on with the tasks at hand. When she is finished, Maureen helps Ann dangle her feet over the edge of the bed. She needs to take it slowly. She's not sure if Ann's strong enough to stand on her own. She lowers the bed so Ann can touch the floor. Slowly but surely, Ann stands. They walk to the bathroom, where Maureen helps Ann into the shower and makes sure she's seated safely on the shower bench. After the shower, she helps Ann get dressed.

"May I sit in a chair?" Ann inquires. "I'd love to eat some breakfast sitting up rather than spilling all over myself and my clean clothes."

"Are you sure you feel up to it? It's really easy to overdue things the first time you get up."

"Actually, the shower was so refreshing, I feel good, weak but good. I'm breathing better than I have in a long time."

Maureen smiles. "I hear that from a lot of heart surgery patients. The grafts done are now restoring blood flow to all areas of the heart and into the rest of your body. You'll start to feel better as more blood can flow through your body. Notice how pink your fingers look."

Ann looks at her hands. They're getting wrinkled, and the arthritis has taken its toll on her finger joints. They're still not bad for a woman her age, she thinks. Her nails have grown since she last inspected her hands. Maureen is right: her hands look pink. She looks down at her feet, and they also look rosy.

"Mom, look what I found: your favourite fresh biscuits, hot out of the oven. I called Amy, and she said I could get you one. So, I bought a couple for me as well." Jake is beaming with his prize.

"It will go perfect with your mother's poached egg." Maureen carries the breakfast tray over to Ann.

It's then that Jake realizes his mother's out of bed. "Hey, you look great. You had a shower, and you're actually wearing the clothes Dad and I brought to you yesterday. Wait till Dad sees you. He's been so worried."

Jake pulls up a chair next to his mother. She eats her breakfast, including the fresh biscuit. He has his biscuits and coffee, while they talk about the latest news and weather reports. Jake tells her more about their evening with the family.

As they sit back to enjoy each other's company, Ann yawns. "That's enough, Mom. You're going to exhaust yourself on the first day. I'll get Maureen to help you back into bed. You need a nap before Dad gets here."

"I think you're right, Son. Can you see if Maureen is free?" Ann suddenly realizes her strength is spent, and she'll require assistance getting back into bed.

With impeccable timing, Maureen arrives. "Ready to get back into bed?" Without waiting for an answer, she helps Ann up and moves her back into bed. After arranging the monitors, she leaves the room as quickly as she popped in.

"Jake, I need you to buy me a couple of gifts for my nurses. I can't think of anything, but maybe you can."

"No problem, Mom. I'll get something and bring it back later today so you've them here." Jake pulls the blankets up around his mother and drops a kiss on her cheek. "Love ya, Mom. See you later."

Ann listens to his steps down the hall. She can tell he must be sending a message on his iPhone and walking. She knows her family's habits well.

Chapter Twenty-Eight

Jake is indeed sending messages, first to his sister to see if she'd spoken with Dr. Morgan and if she had time for breakfast, the second to his office to let his assistant know he'll be in later in the morning. Amy responds immediately. She's just finished speaking with Dr. Morgan and is starving. She's ready for something to eat before rounds and scheduled surgeries later in the morning. He then calls his father to see where he's at and if he wants to meet up. Ed's not far from the hospital. He agrees to meet up in the hospital cafeteria before going up to spend time with Ann.

Jake and Amy get to the cafeteria at the same time. They make their way through the food line and find a table close to the door so they can watch for their father. Ed comes through the door, he sees them, and waves as he heads for the food line.

"You look better than you did when I saw you earlier this morning," Jake says to Amy as he starts to eat his second breakfast of the day.

"It's amazing what a shower and clean clothes with a touch of makeup can do." Amy pops a piece of bacon in her mouth. "Let's wait for Dad, so I can bring you both up to date with my findings." With a mouth full of food, Jake can only nod.

"Good morning my two favourites." Ed always teases that he has a favourite son and a favourite daughter. "You both look bright eyed. You must have gotten some sleep." Ed sets his tray on the table.

"Well, actually, I woke Amy up. She was sleeping in Mom's room on the lounge chair." Jake pitches another fork full of eggs and hash browns into his mouth. A look of alarm passes over Ed.

"No Dad, Mom's fine. I had an emergency and worked so late that I was too exhausted to drive home. I was going to crash on my couch in my office, but as I passed Mom's room, I remembered the sleeper lounge I had delivered to her room just in case you wanted to catch some rest while Mom slept. So, I just dropped there. I don't actually remember my head hitting the pillow. Good thing Jake showed up when he did, or I would have missed my call with Dr. Morgan."

Ed hadn't taken time to eat last night when he got home. He watered his plants and tried to sleep, but he had so many calls. He finally called Joyce and gave her the update and invited her to fan out the information so he could get some rest. He managed a couple of hours sleep, rising early as usual. He made good time through rush hour to get to the hospital.

Since Amy had learned early in med school how to grab food when she could, she's already finished. As the other two eat their breakfast, Amy fills them in on Ann's progress. "Mom's doing well; she was up this morning, had a shower, and is now resting." Amy pulls her mother's monitor up on her phone to check her charts and sets it down in front of her father and Jake so they can see the ticker-tape report running across the small screen. "I had a long chat with Dr. Morgan this morning. Both of us have reviewed Mom's developments. He has suggested I review all the monitor printouts, and I should look for the cause of the irregularities in the heartbeat. Of course, I've already checked the printouts.

The irregularities have settled down in the past eight hours. I correlated the information, and I think I've discovered Mom may have been having a reaction to one of the medications. I have a friend from Johns Hopkins who specializes in drug reactions, so I've spoken to him. He has one of his people checking out the drugs Mom's been given, along with the prescriptions Dr. Benton in Riverside prescribed. He suggested I see about the stuff Mom takes from the health food store. Many people think vitamins are harmless, but when they're combined with other prescribed drugs, they can be lethal."

Jake and Ed finish their breakfast and sip their coffee. Jake nods, "Do you remember when Aunty Katherine and Mom took those cayenne tablets to lower their blood pressure?"

"Perfect example. Aunty passed out in the grocery store because she already had low blood pressure. Those blended vitamins could've killed them. In fact, you'll recall the paramedics couldn't find a pulse when they first found her."

"I can get the names of the vitamins your mother takes and bring it back tomorrow. That is, if she can't remember the names."

"Actually Dad, can you phone Joyce and see which one of them's planning to sneak in and see Mom today?"

"How did you know someone who isn't a direct relative would try that?" Ed flashes his guilt with rosy red cheeks.

"Because I've been around hospitals long enough to be able to spot the rule breakers, and I know Mom and her friends. Just tell any one of them they can't do something, and watch what happens."

Winking at her brother, Amy checks her watch. "Listen, you're my most darling men in the world, and I love talking with you both, but I've got back to work. I have surgery in an hour, and I haven't made rounds yet."

Jake looks at his phone. "Wow, look at the time. I better get to the office as well. By the way, Dad, Mom was up and had breakfast with me. She went back to bed when I left her."

"You have had two breakfasts already!" Ed laughs and shakes his head. Jake's always had an amazing appetite, and his metabolism seems to keep him slim. He was always the smallest kid in school and on the sports teams, and at 5ft8in, he has a slim waist. Maybe it's his appetite that scares women off; it can't be his lack of good looks or charm. Ed's never figured out why his two kids aren't married and providing grandchildren like his brother's and Ann's sister's kids.

"Dad?" Jake realizes his father is not paying attention.

"Sorry, Son. I was thinking."

"I said I've to get to the office. I think we made plans last night with Uncle Owen, Aunty Sara, Uncle Bill, and Aunt Katherine: 5:00 at the Keg, right?"

"Yes, that is the plan." Ed gathers up the food trays and walks toward the drop-off. Jake follows.

"See you then. Oh, by the way, tell Mom I already know what to buy, and I'll bring the gifts and cards later this afternoon. She'll understand." He sees the puzzled look.

"Will do. Have yourself a good day, Son." Ed walks off to the elevators, and Jake moves toward the exit doors to his car. He's checking messages from the office as he walks. Good thing he's got such a good team back at the office, who have managed to pick up the slack. He has to remember to do something nice for each of them. He puts a reminder into his day planner. Normally, he'd have messages filling his cell to capacity, but today, only those messages flagged as high-priority messages are showing up.

Ed stops, he gets a whiff of something good. He follows his nose to the little gift shop: they have fresh peanut butter cookies. He picks up a basket of them and heads up to Ann. He's proud of his transaction, knowing these are a favourite with Ann. On his way up to her room, he dials Joyce and asks her to include a stop on her way. He suggests she shouldn't concern herself with anyone questioning her, since she's making a delivery at Amy's request.

Ed feels like Little Red Riding Hood as he enters Ann's room with his basket of treats. Ann's sitting up, much to his surprise. "I thought you'd be sleeping." Ed reaches out to kiss Ann. With no one else around, he doesn't feel uncomfortable about expressing his love for his wife.

"Hey, do I smell cookies," Ann jokes as she returns his kiss.

"My wife can never be accused of putting romance before food."

"Not when fresh peanut butter cookies are on the line, or more precisely, in the basket.

Ed replays the conversations he's had over breakfast. They share a few jokes over Jake's ability to eat multiple meals, remembering times when he was younger. They're each munching on a cookie when Amy drops in.

Amy had changed into her scrubs. Since Dr. Morgan couldn't be available, she's arranged for Sophia Charter, the hospital administrator and CEO of the board, to come to meet with her to speak with her mother about her diagnosis and prognosis. Always concerned about the rules and transparency she wants to be sure the protocols regarding relatives are covered. She has two other young doctors and Nurse Maureen with her as well.

"Hello Mr. and Mrs. Murray." The formality makes Ed and Ann put down their cookies. Maureen grins behind the doctors. She loves this part of her job. "I want to introduce Dr. Sophia Charter, the hospital administrator and CEO of the hospital board of directors. This is Dr. Ramon and Dr. Kowalski. They're both interns, and they're going to work with me for the next few days on their rotation through all the units here at the hospital."

Both interns are more than a little uncomfortable. Being with the two most powerful women in the hospital is nerve-racking. They had never even met Dr. Charter. It's common knowledge that Dr. Murray is the best in the hospital and that she expects her interns to read the charts and understand the patients before they make rounds. They also know this is the doctor's mother.

Ed excuses himself and stands outside the room, watching from the glass door. He knows Amy is not at her best in front of her parents, but he's pretty sure no one recognizes that fact except for him and Ann.

Dr. Charter starts the conversations, discussing the board position on Amy having her mother as her patient. She explains the consequences of the decision and rules Amy has to follow and why these rules are in place. Ann nods in confirmation that she understands what she is being told. She also skips the fact that she remembers little Sophie Charter from the Booster Mind Team. Once Dr. Charter finishes, Amy explains what they did from the time Ann arrived until this moment. She also explains some of the prognosis, along with the potential risks and complications to the surgeries. Ed listens from the doorway, realizing this meeting's even more important than he first thought. He's intrigued by Dr. Charter and what she has said. It appears both women may have put their careers and jobs on the line for Ann. He had no idea of the consequences of what Amy had done to save her mother.

Dr. Charter finishes up. "Mrs. Murray, it's been a pleasure to meet you again. I wish it had been under different circumstances. You're in the best hands we have. I'm not sure if you remember me but I went to elementary and high school with Amy and Jake."

"Little Sophie? Of course, I do remember you. Your mother and I sat together for many of the special events. You were so sweet; you've grown into such a beautiful woman. Thank you for everything you've done for me. I appreciate it very much." Ann solemnly shakes Dr. Charter's extended hand.

Dr. Charter takes a minute to introduce herself to Ed, who has remained by the door for the entire conversation.

As soon as Dr. Charter leaves the room, the young interns begin to check the incision, while Amy asks them questions about the prognosis, medication requirements, and expectations as to when the patient can go home.

"Dr. Murray, I have reviewed this patient's chart since her admission, and I notice some irregularities in her heartbeat early on, but I see they've decreased. I'm confused by this. Is it a reaction to the meds or something else?" Dr. Kowalski'as done his homework, and Amy's impressed.

"Interesting you caught that. It's been an issue. You could be right, as it appears to be a reaction of some kind, but to be honest, it's quite perplexing. Would you be interested in doing a bit of research into it? I could use some assistance."

"Yes, I would. Research is something I'm seriously considering when I finish my internship."

"Dr. Murray, would you be interested in my help as well?" Dr. Ramon inquires. "I've some personal experience in drug reactions from my own family, and I'm interested in learning more."

"By all means. Let's spend a few minutes on a course of action before my first surgery." Amy's pleased to have both doctors show an interest. They're both very cleaver and show great potential. As busy as she is, she can use the help.

Ed and Ann talk over everything they have heard. They hope all this means Ann's on the mend and can go home soon. Ann's starting to feel better and she's restless. Ed decides he'll bring some books and magazines from home for her to occupy her time.

Chapter Twenty-Nine

With great excitement, Ed helps Ann move out of the ICU room and into a ward later that morning. She's sharing her new room with three other women. Ann takes time to meet each of her roommates, and they share surgery history. One lady has had surgery for bowel cancer, another has had similar heart surgery, and the third woman has just received a hip replacement. Ed chats with the ladies as he helps organize Ann's things in her new room.

Owen and Sara have found her new accommodations and spend a few minutes visiting. Not wanting to tire her, they invite Ed to join them downstairs for coffee. They plan to run a few errands for the day and meet up with Ed, Jake, and Amy for dinner again tonight.

As they left, Katherine pops in. She's had to bring in her daughter for X-rays; it seems she broke her pinkie finger at basketball practice. She spends just a couple of minutes with Ann while Carrie's waiting for a splint. She plans to drop by again later, once she gets Carrie settled at home.

"You sure do move around a lot for someone with a chest full of staples and stitches," Joyce announces as she sweeps into Ann's room with her arms full.

"Good grief. What have you brought half my house?" Ann couldn't believe the size of the box Joyce's carrying.

"Well, I brought you in some things from your place that I knew Ed's probably not thought you might like to have. Also, this is the stuff Amy wanted me to bring for her. I had no idea your medicine shelf was so full of vitamins and health food stuff. Since I didn't know what you actually take and what you thought about but never got around to taking, I just brought it all." Joyce sets the box down and goes to hug her best friend. "Do you know how much I have missed you? You gave me quite a fright."

Ann chuckles. "I like to keep people on their toes." She eyes the box. "My cupboard must look pretty bare. I'd no idea it had so much stuff in it."

"Just you and me? Where's Ed? I thought you might have a room full of company. I was practising my excuses that would get me into your room. It was a real panic. My heart dropped into my feet when I slid open the door of the ICU number that Ed gave me. The bed's empty, and housecleaning's stripping it all down. A nice nurse named Maureen gave me directions to find you." Joyce could talk a mile a minute when nervous or excited.

"Actually, I did have company earlier. Ed went down to the cafeteria with his brother and sister-in-law. My sister just left. They're all meeting up at the Keg later today to have dinner with Amy and Jake."

"Well, the Keg, eh. I might just have to crash that party."

"No need to crash; I'd love to have you join us." Ed spooks her as he quietly enters the room.

"You take all the fun out of things." Joyce turns and hugs him. "Good to see you."

"Owen and Sara are going over to the mall. Apparently Sara has a list of things she needs to pick up. They'll pop back later."

Ed looks over at the box. "Unbelievable. Look at that box. It's quite the collection you brought in. Ann, do you take all those vitamins?"

"Well, first the box is not full of vitamins. Joyce brought me a few things she thought I might need," Ann defends herself. "If you bring it over and put it here beside me on the bed, we can sort through it."

Ed picks up the box and puts it beside Ann. As she visits with Joyce, she puts the vitamins she uses on the bed stand. Ed puts her change of night-clothes and underwear and a bag containing an outfit in the empty drawer next to the bed. He sets her books and notebook, along with a mystery novel, on top of the bed stand. Joyce sits down and catches them up on the latest happenings in the neighborhood.

Ann lies back in the bed, exhausted from her task. "The rest is garbage, and you can set it aside to take back home and put into the bin."

"OK. I'll send a message to Amy and see if she wants to send her two nice doctors to pick up this stuff." Ed carefully punches keys on his phone. "I think she might still be in surgery."

"Actually, I mentioned to Maureen that I was the messenger, and she said she'd let the doctors know. She thought they might drop by shortly."

Right on cue, Dr. Kowalski rounds the corner. "I think you were talking about me," he smiles.

"Perfect timing." Ed moves so the doctor could move in closer to Ann. Ed introduces Dr. Kowalski to Joyce.

"OK, let's go through this stuff, and I'll take a few notes. You need to tell me how often and how many of each you take."

Dr. Kowalski looks like a police detective as he takes notes and asks questions. When he's finished, Ed decides to go for a walk so Ann and Joyce can spend some time together. He knows Joyce has been very worried about her best friend, and he knows Ann could use some new company. He's found a sunny little family sitting room down the hall that seems to be a great spot for a little afternoon nap.

"You two visit, I'll be back later." He pecks Ann on the cheek and heads off.

Joyce moves her chair closer to the bed, and as Ed leaves, the two are already whispering and joking. It is good to see Ann starting to look so much better. He knows with the progress he's witnessed today, he should be able to get a good night's sleep.

Chapter Thirty

Amy stops by the mini lab just down the corridor from her office. Len Kowalski and Stu Ramon sit in front of two computer screens, with a very large and impressive electronic microscope separating them. They continue to run tests on the reactions of the various medications and vitamins.

"Any luck, doctors?" Amy walks around the counter to face Stu and Len.

"A couple of interesting discoveries. Not one of the vitamins has shown a reaction to any of the drugs Mrs. Murray's taken during her stay here." Stu leans back in his chair to stretch his muscles.

Amy chews her bottom lip. "OK, that in itself is good to know."

"Well, here's where it gets interesting," Len jumps in. "There are three bottles with combined vitamins. Vitamin A, C, and D are all contained in various dosages in these three multi-type vitamins. On their own, none of the vitamins really cause much problem. However," he brings his information up on the big screen so all three can review it, "when you add up the recommended daily dosage of each bottle and each capsule, which is what the patient's been taking on a daily basis, you can see a concern starting to develop. By taking them together, they actually exceed the body's requirements by almost three times. This wouldn't be an issue for anyone with a problem of high blood pressure, but Mrs. Murray's medical records suggest her blood pressure has been very stable over the past twenty years or so, but on the lower end of the normal scale."

Stu continues from this point. "With her tendency for lower blood pressure, by taking the combination of these vitamins, she causes her heart to develop an irregular heartbeat. In fact, it's actually pausing, and that's what was creating the irregularities. More important, it may have helped to put her into cardiac arrest. That might have indirectly saved her life. With the condition of the coronary arteries at the time of the bypass surgeries, if this hadn't happened, she may not have recognized her symptoms until it was too late."

Amy shudders at the thought. "I have seen so many harmful effects from people misusing vitamins. So many think they're harmless. I can't believe my own mother didn't consult with me before she took these." Ann shakes her head in disbelief.

"I rechecked the printouts from the monitors. I wonder if the irregular heartbeats continued until the vitamins started to deplete in her system. You can see where the changes are now erratic but actually have a pattern. It suggests to me that as the volume decreased in her body, so do the irregular beats. If you follow this thought process, see the results to my theory." Stu comments as he types a command, and this information comes up on the large screen.

"You know, this makes better sense than a reaction to the meds. Are there any documented case studies to prove this hypothesis?" Amy's curious if anyone has already put together these two factors. She's always amazed to learn something so simple and yet so new. The medical institution likes to believe it knows and has done everything.

Stu has already started the search. "I haven't found any case studies yet, but I'll run the program over the remainder of the evening through the international case study database. If there is anything, we should have something before your evening rounds."

"Great. As soon as you get anything, just let me know." Amy leaves the room with a positive frame of mind. She doesn't want to get too excited until she runs the results past Dr. Morgan and her friend at John Hopkins. She needs to get to her computer so she can forward him the reports she has just reviewed with Stu and Len.

As she walks to her office, her appointment reminder beeps. She checks her phone. Unbelievably, it is her reminder that it is almost time to meet her father and brother at the Keg for dinner. She realizes she hasn't eaten since breakfast. She grabs a bottle of water out of her small office refrigerator and quickly sends off a message with the attachments to Dr. Morgan. Hopefully, he'll get back to her by morning.

Amy splashes her face with water, runs a brush through her mass of natural waves, and applies a quick dash of makeup. She changes out of her scrubs into her street clothes; Amy's office has a large closet, and she has it stocked with a good supply of outfits.

Just as she finishes, her office phone rings. It's Jake. "I'm in Mom's room. Did you want to pop in, and we can walk to the Keg together?"

Amy feels guilty. She's been in surgery all afternoon and hasn't seen her mother since rounds this morning. Surgery days are always hectic. She did know that Ann's in a ward room. Amy had tried to get her into a private room, but the hospital's short of beds, so she couldn't make it happen. "Sure, give me five minutes, and I'll meet you in Mom's room."

Ann checks her messages and dashes off down the passage to the elevator. She thinks about her conversations earlier with Len and Stu. Perhaps she'll try to find some funds to do a study on this issue. She's in deep thought when she reaches the elevator and walks straight into her father. Startled, she looks up to see him grin.

"You were concentrating so hard, you didn't notice me. I was on my way to your office. I thought I'd meet you, and we could walk together."

"I'm just on my way down to Mom's room to meet you." Arm and arm, they walk down the corridor.

"Hi guys, I haven't eaten since breakfast so I'm looking forward to getting a bite at the Keg."

Amy remains behind, while Joyce, her father, and brother wait outside the room. The rest of her visitors left earlier to give Ann some much-needed rest. She checks her mother's monitor. "Mom, you look exhausted. You've got to start telling people when you're tired. Otherwise, you're slowing down your progress," Amy lectures her mother. "I love you and want to get you healthy and back home."

"You're right. I'm so tired. It's just so great to see everyone. I didn't realize how draining it is. It was only a couple of people at a time, so I just didn't think about being tired."

"Mom, you've never had to pace yourself. But believe me, I'm speaking from experience, you need to learn, especially now, because when you get home I'm not going to be there to bully you and send people home." Amy leans over and kisses her mom. She makes a mental note to discuss this issue at dinner tonight. "Now, see about getting a little rest before your dinner comes. Is there anything you want me to bring you back?"

"Think of me at dessert." Ann winks at her daughter. They both share a sweet tooth. Chocolate desserts have been a special mother–daughter treat they've participated in quite regularly over the years. Their secret's never been exposed on their hips, perhaps because of their busy schedules and great metabolism.

As the four walked to the restaurant for dinner, Amy explains the need for rest when recovering from heart surgery. "I know Mom thinks she's in control when it comes to things, but this time, Dad, I'm relying on you and Joyce. You guys have to run roughshod over her to make sure she rests properly. Otherwise, she's going to be back here … or worse."

"Your father and I have already started to set up a schedule to tag team this. We'll take turns being around to make sure there is never too much company." Joyce advises.

"And too many phone calls," chimes in Jake. "You know how much time Mom spends talking to people on the phone."

Nodding in agreement, Ed and Joyce begin to discuss how they can make it work. With Ed trying to answer the phone in the evenings and mornings, Joyce can handle the daytime. She's already planned to prepare the meals and clean when Ann gets home.

Jake voices his suggestion. "Maybe we can start calling Mom's friends and the relatives now to explain no telephone calls over ten minutes and visits have to be scheduled through one of you. No drop-in visitors."

"I know it may seem mean, but sometimes serious issues call for serious measures, and Mom's too kind and thoughtful to think she might be hurting someone's feelings." Amy continued, "It's been one of the hardest things for me to learn, how to say no. The first few times, I'm telling you right now, Mom's going to be mad, but she'll get glad as she realizes her health has to be a priority right now."

Over dinner, they discuss this further with the family. All are in agreement, acknowledging they had seen Ann starting to wilt, which was why they had left. Again, they share a lovely time laughing together.

Amy leaves an hour later. "Sorry folks, it may be Friday night for your guys facing a weekend off, but for me, it's just another night. I've got patients to check before I can call it a night."

Amy leaves the hospital at a decent hour, looking forward to an uneventful night with a luxurious bubble bath and a good sleep in her own bed. On the weekends, Amy normally drops by the hospital to do rounds and then returns home to putter around. Today, she stops in to visit her mother after rounds. Ann's healing nicely and getting stronger each day. Amy expects she'll be sending her mother home either Monday or Tuesday.

She meets Cheryl on Saturday afternoon. Cheryl's agreed to get Amy's house in order and put some seriously needed design touches in it. Amy's excited to have her place look like a home so she can invite her family and friends in for dinner and an evening together. She gives a set of the keys to Cheryl, along with a cheque to cover expenses. They've agreed on a budget for furniture, paint, and accessories for each room. Amy calls the storage company to have her furniture she inherited from her grandparents delivered during the week so she and Cheryl can decide on what additional furniture Amy'll need. She's gone to the storage unit to look at the inventory, but the shipping crates have never been opened. Amy's excited to have the time to look through the boxes. It's like Christmas. The task of decorating her house to become her home is now in good hands and Amy's happy to hand the job off to Cheryl, knowing she loves these kinds of projects. Amy knows Cheryl's husband, Bert, will be glad it's someone else's house and not their house for a change.

On Sunday afternoon, Amy drops by to check up on her mother. Amy discusses the plans she and Cheryl have come up with in detail with her mother, who loves every minute and is looking forward to a visit to the house. Amy has taken both Ann and Ed to the house before she bought it, but Ann hasn't been there since Amy took possession.

Chapter Thirty-One

Bright and early Monday morning, Amy meets Len and Stu in her office to go over the results of their study into the vitamins Ann's been taking. They've found several case studies with direct correlation to Ann's irregular heat beat. Amy's already discussed the results with Dr. Morgan, and they agree this is most likely the culprit. As a result of their hard work, Amy extends Dr. Morgan's invitation for the two young doctors to present their findings at his next monthly cardiologist meeting in Edmonton. Both doctors are thrilled at such a prestigious opportunity. Amy offers her services to preview their presentation.

She reviews her patient charts and starts her rounds, armed with the good news that her mother can go home a day earlier than expected. Stu and Len are still with her department for another week, so they join her on rounds. Amy sees these two doctors hold great potential, especially for working with difficult cases. She makes a note to call to a friend who could use these two on his team. His trauma centre at Massachusetts General is one of the best in North America. She visited the centre and the cardiology department last year at a conference and was very impressed. She hates to see such talent leave the province, but she also knows their abilities need to be developed, and her friend is the perfect teacher.

Amy checks her mother's incision. The staples have been removed, and things are healing nicely. Ann will have a nasty scar for some time, but if she takes care, she can start to apply a cream to lessen the scar. It'll certainly never go away and will be a constant reminder to Ann to take care of and listen to her body.

"Mom, I'm going to take a couple of safety precautions. I want to monitor your heart rate for the next couple of weeks. The monitor's in a bra that you'll wear round the clock. Inside this bra are fabric sensors. The small microprocessor continuously monitors the EKG and heart rate. It sends a signal to a small receiver, which will be located in your cell phone. Your phone will forward the information to my computer in my office. You can take this receiver out of the bra so you can wash the bra. Just follow the instructions, and you'll be fine. In fact, I'm sending you home with three bras and one receiver to make it easier on you."

Ann's ecstatic at the prospects of going home. Amy explains it's conditional on her mother's promise that she'll not take a vitamin or any other medication, not even an aspirin, without first checking with Amy. She'll also have to wear the monitoring bra all the time.

Amy leaves her mother to take her shower and get dressed. "I'll be back in about an hour to check you out. Dad's usually here by then, so you can surprise him if you like, or I can call him?"

"No, let's just surprise him. As much as he complains about not liking surprises, I know he'll love this one. I can't wait until he sees me dressed."

Ann starts getting dressed. She puts on the new bra; it fits very well. But when she puts on her clothes, she realizes she has a problem. She knows she's lost some weight, but she looks like she's trying to wear her big sister's clothes. That would be fine if she had a big sister. Her roommates share her joke, as they, too, have lost significant weight. Ann decides she needs to find a scale. So, off she goes, holding up her pants for fear she'll expose herself if she's not careful.

When she returns, Ann checks her drawer, remembering Joyce has brought her a change of street clothes. Maybe they'll fit better. Ann opens the bag and sees that Joyce's actually bought her a new outfit. Much to her amazement, the pants and top fit like a glove, showing off her new body. Not wanting to wrinkle her new clothes by crawling back into bed, she sits in the lounge chair to rest and chat with her newfound friends and roommates. She's written their names and contact information into her notebook and plans to call them in a few weeks, once they're also home.

"Wow, look at you." Ed's surprised to see his wife dressed in street clothes and not in her nightgown and bathrobe.

"Amy tells me I can go home," Ann blurts out. She'd wanted to act nonchalant, but her excitement has gotten the best of her.

"Well, in that case, I'll pack you up and we can leave."

"I need to go back to the ICU. I have cards I want to leave for Maureen and Emily." Jake had remembered to get her two small gifts to give to her two nurses. He bought gift cards for the hospital staff's favourite local restaurant, the Keg, so each of the women could take a friend or their husband out for dinner. It's in a nice little envelope. Ann's given her numerous fruit baskets and flowers to the staff at the nursing station on a daily basis. There wouldn't have been enough room for the flowers and certainly not enough people to eat all the treats in the baskets. She'd also given several to the nurses to give to other patients at the hospital. Ann's kept all of the cards and she'll send thank you notes once she got home.

Ed packs up her things and takes them to the car, while Ann goes over to ICU. Emily's working; she's pleased to see how well Ann's progressed. She expresses her gratitude for the card and takes Maureen's to give to her later that day. Ann hugs her and goes back to her room to wait for Ed. Not surprisingly, Ed's waiting for her. Amy's dropped back with a couple of prescriptions and list of dos and don'ts for her mother to follow, including some menu and food choices.

Ann protests at the sight of a wheelchair. "Sorry, Mom, it's the rules."

Ed pushes the wheelchair. Amy walks along with her parents. When they get to the elevator, Amy promises she'll be out on the weekend. She'll call every day to see how things are going. Ed winks at his daughter; he has already worked out a schedule and plan with Joyce. Amy'll check in later to see how the plan is working.

Amy breathes a sigh of relief. She's glad her mother has survived and is able to return home. She knows that eventually both her parents will die; she is, after all, a medical professional, and death is part of life. But, as a daughter, she wants her parents to live forever.

Chapter Thirty-Two

Joyce welcomes Ann into the house. Every room is full of flower arrangements. Ann jokes at the amount of business her friends at the flower shop have done.

"I didn't thank you for this gorgeous outfit. I thought you'd brought me something from my closet. How did you know to get something so small?"

"Remember, my mother had heart problems. She lost tons of weight, so I figured you would, too."

Tears run down Ann's cheeks. It's all too much for her; coming back home, when she thought she'd never return, and seeing all these flowers and her best friend.

"OK, when tears come, it's a sure sign you're exhausted. You need to lie down for a while to rest. Joyce is in charge of meals but I think you need a rest. That snack at Peter's Drive Inn should tide you over for a little while."

"Yes, I did manage to pack away his regular loaded burger with most of the onion rings and quite a bit of my favourite pineapple shake."

"I see you're already following Amy's plan for healthy meals," Joyce snorts. "I'll get you back on her plan at dinner."

"I'm looking forward to your cooking; the staff at the hospital could use some lessons from you." Ann hugs her friend and lets Ed march her off to the bedroom. She has to admit the drive home has been more tiring than she'd expected.

Three hours later, Ann opens her eyes. She looks around and realizing she's in her own bed, she stretches and catches herself as her chest muscles remind her they're not quite ready for that kind of workout. Without the benefit of the hospital bed aids, Ann struggles to get up. She finally figures out she needs to roll over and off the side of the bed. Once she tries this, she quickly finds herself up. She can smell food, and it smells amazing. She follows her nose out to the kitchen. Joyce and Ed are sitting at the kitchen island, sipping lemonade.

"I didn't realize how tired I was." Ann yawns.

Pouring Ann a glass of lemonade Ed directs her to the eating nook in the kitchen, Joyce replies, "Perfect timing since dinner's just now finished. You, as always, have perfect timing."

That is not the case, but Ann smiles. It's so good to be home.

Ed sets the table while Joyce dishes up her meal. After grace, they start to eat. "This looks incredible. Joyce you have really outdone yourself, and I'm starving." Ed's already busy piling the food on his plate. He's oblivious to the looks Ann and Joyce have just exchanged while dishing up their plates.

"Only had a couple of small snacks, eh?" Ann inquires.

"Exactly," Ed replies with a mouth full of food.

Joyce changes the subject. "I know your fiftieth anniversary is right around the corner." Ed looks liked a deer in the headlights of a car. Joyce continues, "I spoke with Amy and Jake about it, and if it's OK with you two, I think that maybe you should consider having a simple little dinner over in Huntersville with just your relatives and a few friends."

"Actually, I've been thinking about it at the hospital, and I made a couple of lists." Joyce and Ed roll their eyes. Ignoring their looks, Ann goes on. "I agree, it's too much work. Even if I hadn't had this surgery, I've been thinking about something very easy and simple for all of us. Amy and Jake are both busy, and I can't ask them to take more time from their jobs to help me, especially after what they've done these past few days."

"Great, after we eat, let's go outside and sit on the deck to enjoy the summer. We can go over your lists. Ed and I sat outside earlier, and it's so beautiful. The entire yard's in bloom. I wish Al could like yard work as much as he loves golf."

"I'm truly blessed that Ed is not a true-blue fan of golf."

"Oh, I like the odd game with Al, Bert, and Bruce, but my skills leave so much to be desired. It's actually a game of annoyance and frustration. Not exactly my cup of tea. But fortunately, it's not their greatest skill, either." Ed smiles. "Puttering around the yard's so much more rewarding, and I don't have to keep score."

Once they finish dinner, they refresh their glasses of lemonade and move to the deck. It's such a beautiful day, and the air's still very warm. Joyce has found Ann's notebook with her lists. Armed with her own book, the three sit, enjoying the day and the company. Ann had indeed kept her plans for the day very low key, nothing at all resembling their twenty-fifth anniversary party. Surprisingly, there are only forty-two names on her list, all very close friends and only their immediate family.

"I don't want an open house at all. No one ever listens to the no gift rule, and we really don't need anything else in this house." Ed's emphatic.

Ann agrees. "I think we should just book the Flames's private dinning room, have a wonderful meal, share some laughs, jokes, and a couple of hours of company, and call it a day." Joyce's pleasantly pleased. Her friends really do intend to keep their anniversary low key.

The telephone interrupts their discussion. It's Amy, checking in on her mother. Since Joyce answered the phone, Amy inquires on calls. Joyce answers in cryptic messages. "Everything's quiet this afternoon. Your mom's had a good nap, and we just finished dinner."

"Probably because no one knows she's home yet," Amy suggests.

"You're right on that. Would you like to speak to your mom? I think she misses seeing you already. I'm leaving shortly for home so your mom can go to bed at a good time. Otherwise, Al will think I've abandoned him." With that, Joyce hands the phone over to Ann. She hopes Amy got the message to call her later at her house. She expects tomorrow might be busy. Sooner or later, their friends'll know Ann's back home, and they'll all be eager to see her. Each one will only stay for a few minutes; it's the number of them that's the problem.

Ann spends the next few minutes answering Amy's questions regarding her health. She explains their tentative plans for the anniversary. Amy's pleased to hear the plans and agrees to call Jake later. Ann loves the new phones they've recently purchased. It allows her to speak with five or six people at the same time, so it'll be great fun to plan things with Jake and Amy. It also has big numbers, so Ed doesn't have to put on his reading glasses to dial the phone. He can also check who's calling with the same ease.

While Ann finishes her conversation with Amy, Ed excuses himself to water plants. He wants to make sure he's in the house for the remainder of the evening to handle the usual calls from their family. Sometimes, he misses having a big extended family of aunts, uncles, and cousins, but this is one of those times where less is definitely better.

While Ed waters his plants, Joyce tidies up the kitchen and sets up a small snack for Ann to have later in the evening. Joyce wants to make sure Ann has no reason to be tempted to do something strenuous. The house is immaculate, and the laundry's done. Nothing Ann can think of needs to be done. Her only job is to sit back and get better.

Amy's papers include some menu ideas, and it suggests half-dozen smaller meals and snacks to start building back Ann's strength. No greasy fried foods, plenty of fruits and vegetables, fish and chicken, nuts and grains, and hearty amounts of carbohydrates. No salt. Joyce and Ed have reviewed the foods, and between them, they designed a menu with food choices both Ed and Ann like. Joyce made the list, and Ed went shopping. The fridge is now packed with food.

Over the next few days, Ann's strength and energy slowly start to return. It's not long before she can walk to the end of the block. The plans for their anniversary have started to take shape, and Joyce is finding fewer excuses to be at the house.

Ann complains about the lack of clothes that fit, even though she's regained a few pounds. They decide that on Friday, she and Joyce will plan a trip to her favourite shop in Huntersville. Ed and Al will join them. They plan to go for lunch at the Flames and then meet with the events coordinator to complete the plans for the anniversary. Lunch is great, and while Ed and Al decide to go over to the hardware and garden store, Joyce and Ann leave for the dress shop. They'll meet back at the restaurant for tea and dessert.

Ann finds several outfits very quickly, including a nice evening suit for their anniversary party. By the time she's tried them on, she's ready to go home. Ann complains her favourite pastime has worn her out. She does manage enough energy for a piece of the Flame's pecan ganache, made with dark chocolate and whipping cream. It's definitely not on Amy's list, but Ann's kept to her diet plan all week, and this is her reward.

Chapter Thirty-Three

Jake feels like a burglar. He has waited for everyone to leave. His mission is to get in and out as fast as he can and not get caught.

He's careful to leave everything as he found it. He gets what he needs, making several trips, putting packages in the trunk of his car.

He finishes up and quickly drives away before he's spotted.

Chapter Thirty-Four

Time flies by, and before Ann has too much time to think about it, it's the morning of their fiftieth anniversary. Ann wakes up to Ed staring at her. She smiles. "A penny for your thoughts."

"Well, I've been thinking about the first morning I woke up next to you."

"It was in a small motel just on the outskirts of Edmonton," Ann remembers. "We drove there from the wedding. I was still in my wedding dress. The clerk gave us his best room."

"Yep. Cost $40.00 for the room. It was pretty old, but to me, it was a palace. I only saw you and nothing else." Ed pulls her into his arms. "I'm so lucky we've had such a great life. I wouldn't have changed a minute. I never want to think about life without you."

The telephone interrupts the moment. Ed reaches over to pick up the phone and hands it to Ann. "If we don't answer it, Amy'll have the ambulance over here." He smiles.

Amy's on the phone. "I'm just leaving Calgary," Amy warns. "Are you going to be ready when I get there?"

"Of course. I'm just going to have my shower now. I'll be waiting." Ann moves out of bed to get started. It's going to be a full day.

While Ann is busy getting ready, Ed makes her favourite breakfast: bacon, eggs, and hash browns; Amy's dietary recommendation list has been pushed to the side for the day. Amy plans on picking her up, and they'll be off to the salon for the full deal, as Ed calls it, pedicures, manicures, and hairdos.

Ed and Ann eat breakfast together. They've enjoyed facing each other for fifty years, and Ed's hoping for at least another ten or so. He thinks he's pretty realistic, given Ann's incredible progress. Even Amy's impressed with how well she's been following orders and getting her strength back.

Jake and Amy show up together. Jake only stays for a few minutes. He tells his parents he has some pressing matters, and he'll be back later. It seems strange; Ed notices Jake's been acting very strange lately, but Ed's been so focussed on Ann he's let it go. Amy, on the other hand, is in a hurry to get going. Neither has the time to stop and eat breakfast.

Amy and Ann are ready to leave. Each kisses Ed on a cheek and promise they'll back in a couple of hours. Ed remembers how long their usual full deal takes. They've got lots of time, since dinner isn't for several hours. Ed heads out to water his plants and check the trees. The fruit's so plentiful the branches on the old apple tree almost touch the ground. He's afraid the weight will bring down a few branches. Ed takes off several pieces of fruit and disposes them into the recycle bin.

Just then, Owen shows up with Trevor. "Can you round up another player? We can head over to Crossville for a round of golf and stop for lunch at the clubhouse." Trevor hops out of the car and walks over to his Uncle Ed.

"Let me give Al a call. He's usually ready, willing, and able to golf any time, day or night." Ed jokes.

"Good motto to live by." Trevor hugs his uncle. "It's been a while. You're getting shorter."

"Well, that's what happens when you get old, the body starts to slow down and shrink." Ed pulls his cell out of his pocket and dials Al.

Al's over in just a couple of minutes, pulling his clubs behind him. "I was hoping to find someone for a golf game today. Joyce thought I should be busy; but quite frankly, I'm not sure what I'm supposed to be busy doing. Time's a wasting. Let's get moving." Al's anxious to get moving before Joyce actually finds him something to be busy doing.

While they walk the golf course, all four of them reminisce about their versions of getting ready for their own wedding. They laugh and joke as they enjoy the game and their fellowship together.

As Ed and the men enjoy their round of golf, Amy and her mother are enjoying themselves at the spa. Amy's so pleased to see how well her mother looks. She's kept close track of the monitor, as it files a continuous report to Amy's computer. Her system's programmed to alert her if there are any irregularities. So far, things look very good. They spend the time discussing Amy's house renovations. Cheryl's been working hard at her design business, but she's been getting ready to retire. She's actually hired a young woman to help, with hopes she'll soon be ready and willing to take over Cheryl's small shop.

Chapter Thirty-Five

The morning and early afternoon speed by, and it's almost time to leave for dinner. Amy and Ann have changed into their new outfits. While the styles are very different, they have again managed to find similar colours. Since she was a little girl, Amy's loved dressing in matching outfits with her mother. To this day, their colour choices and styles are often very similar. They joke about going into separate stores on separate days and managing to bring home nearly identical colours and styles. Both women love simple lines and traditional fashions.

Ann found a very simple and elegant couture pantsuit in soft and flowing chiffon and silk, with bursts of sparkles and shiny embossing thread in the jacket. Its pale peach colour flatters Ann's face and brings out the golden grey highlights in her hair. It's amazing that her hair has only a splatter of grey, especially at her age; her natural dark blonde hair has certainly taken its time to age. Ann's friends have always teased her as the grey has finally come in; years after the others had turned to salon assistance to delay the aging process.

Amy found her outfit in the city. It has a flowing skirt and a top in a darker shade of peach. The variegated peach tones are accented with brown and gold and cascades from her slim waist. The top has a gentle cowl neck, which she has accented with a simple gold heart pendant, a gift from her parents on her twenty-first birthday.

Not to be outdone, Ed looks dashing in his new steel-grey suit. Ann found a tie with gold and peach colours to match her outfit. Jake looks elegant in his black suit.

The Murray family looks stunning, and the photographer takes several pictures of the group before they leave for the restaurant. Ann didn't wanted to bother with professional pictures, but Sara and Katherine refused to take no as an answer.

Katherine's made corsages for the women and lapel flowers for the men. She's also taken several arrangements to the Flames. It's her small gift to her big sister, and she knows the white rose arrangements will mean the world to both Ed and Ann. They're almost identical to the arrangements she made for their twenty-fifth anniversary.

The private dinning room is decked out with flowers and candles on all the tables. Joyce's arranged for a small two-layered cake with gold trim and a humorous older bride and groom leaning on each other and sharing a cane instead of a bridal bouquet. In spite of the simplistic plans, the room looks amazing. Ann and Ed stand at the door to welcome their guests. Jake's arranged a small stereo system and has made up a series of songs to play softly in the background throughout the evening. He'll need the music for the gift Amy and Jake have gotten for their parents.

The room fills up quickly, and Jake takes over the responsibilities of the MC for the evening. It doesn't take much to get the evening started. After grace, the servers bring in the various courses. Jake keeps the evening moving and counts on Al, Bruce, and Bert to provide the laughs for the evening. They're more than willing to provide the stories and fun. They've known Ann and Ed for so long, they have a variety of tales.

As the dinner winds down, Ann's favourite ganache dessert is served with tea and coffee. The anniversary cake will be cut up later in the evening, and everyone will take home cake in a small gift box.

"I'd like to ask my sister to join me. We hope everyone will sit back and enjoy our gift to our parents." With that, Jake has the lights lowered, and a screen drops down from the ceiling at the front of the room. Amy adjusts the speakers so the volume's louder, and everyone can hear and see their story.

"Amy and I have worked together to put the story of our parents into this presentation. Just so you know, my job was to act like as a burglar and break into their house to steal my mom's photo albums. As you can imagine, I practically needed to rent a U-haul to move them all. I want to thank Joyce and Al for getting both Mom and Dad out of the house that day and for Joyce to keep them from looking at old pictures. My skills didn't allow me to try to break in after dark, so it was daring daylight burglary. Thank you to all the neighbours who didn't call the police on me."

Jake passes the mic over to his sister to continue. "My job was to take the albums and pick out my favourite pictures to describe their fifty years together. They say a picture is worth a thousand words, and Mom has millions of words in her albums." Amy smiles over at her parents neither are sure what to expect next. "Jake and I have spent most of our evenings working on this. But it's been a burden of love, first because we love our parents so much and second, because neither Jake nor I have much of a social life. We loved looking through all the pictures, and it's been really hard to make the choices on what should be put into this presentation and what should be left out. But here's our portrait of our parents' married lives together."

As the music comes on, Amy's voice is heard over the pictures and the music, as one by one, the pictures flash up on the screen. Jake takes his turn, as he brings in some comic relief to various pictures and stories. Their presentation lasts about an hour. It's been difficult for them to put so much life into such a short time.

When the presentation is finished, the room explodes in cheers and clapping. Next comes the tinkle of glass, and Ed and Ann stand up and respond with a loving kiss. Amy and Jake hand over a beautifully bound book to their parents. Inside, along with all the wonderful pictures neatly displayed on dozens of pages, sits a small holder where the tiny disk is stored.

Jake hands the microphone to his mother. "This has been the perfect finish to a lovely day. I didn't realize my children had such potential for the film industry." Everyone laughs. "I want to thank all of you, our closest relatives and friends, for coming to help us celebrate our fiftieth anniversary. I know you've enjoyed catching up with each other as well. I was not sure I'd be here, but special thanks to God, my doctor, and her great staff, I've made it this far. How much further depends on the grace of God, but I have faith He will send for me when it's my time. For now, I plan to continue to enjoy life every day like it's my last. My prayer for each of you is to do the same thing. It's amazing how much your life changes when you have that outlook."

Ann passes the microphone to Ed. "Like my beautiful bride, I want to thank you all for sharing our special day. Each of you have contributed something special, and I appreciate everything you've done, from helping Ann keep her lists under control right through to getting us here on time. We love each and every one of you with all our hearts. Now, to our children: we need the albums back, because that's how we planned to spend our evening." Ed winked at Ann and again everyone applauds.

"To our two great children, we've been so richly blessed by both of you. You outdid yourselves with your gift to us. I hope you also made copies for yourselves, because we're not going to share this one with you. We still have cake to cut, so don't leave yet." With that, Ed hugs both children and hands the microphone back to Jake.

Joyce has organized a special gift box for each guest. It was her gift to share with everyone. After Ann and Ed cut the cake and all the cake-cutting pictures have been taken, she takes over and packages each box with a piece of cake and a picture of the happy couple. Ann and Ed pass the boxes to each person, along with more hugs.

It has been a great evening, with every waistline increased. By the time the last party guest leaves, it's very late. Amy and Jake drop off their parents at the house and head back to the city.

Chapter Thirty-Six

Ed's up early the next morning. He leaves Ann sound to sleep. He noticed she looked extremely tired by the time they got home. Jake and Amy drove back to the city, so once again, the house is quiet.

A basket with an oversized bow sits on the corner of the counter in the kitchen; it's stacked full of cards. Once Ed has his cup of coffee, he bypasses the basket and focuses on the book Amy and Jake gave them last night. He sits, peacefully flipping page after page of the story of their lives together.

As he sits, he thinks about Ann and her health. He's seen a change over the past few days. It's a change he's not happy with, but as his faith in God is strong, he knows it's not his plan that counts. He knows he's not as smart as his daughter, the doctor, but he has to admit to himself that Ann's not as strong or as healthy as she lets on. He knows sooner or later he'll have to come to grips with the fear that he may have to face the remainder of his life on earth without his beloved wife. He has every faith that Ann, true to her form, will leave him with lists to guide him in the future. In the silence of the morning, he thanks God for always being there for them and for continuing to be with both of them until they each complete their final journey.

Ed is deep in thought and prayer when Ann tiptoes up to him and whispers in his ear, "A penny for your thoughts."

He smiles. "Did you have a good sleep? You were sleeping like a log, so I thought you must be really tired."

Yawning, Ann replies, "It was a full day for an old gal like me."

Ed gets up and wraps his arms around her tiny frame. "You look just as gorgeous as the day I first laid eyes on you."

Ann snuggles in his strong arms for a while. "As much as I love cuddling with you, we are going to be late for church."

Reluctantly, Ed lets her go. "We have time for breakfast. What can I make for you—and don't answer cake." Without waiting for an answer, Ed heads for the stove. Breakfast is his favourite meal of the day and he's already planned for ham and eggs. He has everything ready and moves around the stove, preparing his pièce de résistance. Ann's focus goes to the basket. She pulls out all the cards and organizes them in neat piles. Then, she starts to open each card and read it aloud to Ed as he works.

"Breakfast is served." Ed brings two plates to the breakfast nook.

"We can finish these cards after church." Ann sets the cards aside and puts the envelopes into the recycle container. "Tomorrow I need to get thank you cards to send out to everyone. It's going to take me a couple of days, but I've started a list so I don't forget anyone. Do you want to look at the list for me?" Ann picks up her toast.

"No, I know you. You never forget a list or a person or job for the list."

"Well, I did have heart surgery," Ann jokes.

"Yes, but it was heart not brain surgery, so I trust your memory way more than mine."

Changing the subject, Ed goes on. "I was looking at the book Jake and Amy gave us last night. They must have spent hours on it. It really is our life together in pictures and wonderful stories."

"They did an amazing job, I never expected anything, and to have such a commanding production on their part, I still have trouble finding the words to express my astonishment at what they did. I should've known they were up to something. It's not like them not to show up at least part of the weekend for a meal."

Ed chuckles. "You're right. It's not like our kids to miss your Sunday dinner. I'm thinking maybe we go out for Chinese tonight instead of you cooking something. What do you think?"

"Sounds great. I just have to go brush my teeth and get dressed. I'll be out in a couple of minutes. Looks like you're ready. You must have been up early."

Ed didn't bother to reply, as Ann's already down the hallway. He checks the time: just enough to tidy up the kitchen. He's glad Ann agreed to go out, as she's pale. He'll try to get a couple minutes later in the day to check in with Amy. Amy had given Ann permission not to wear the monitor bra earlier last week, and he needs to figure out how to get Ann to wear it so Amy can check. He shakes his head. Maybe he's just becoming too much of an old worrywart.

Chapter Thirty-Seven

The next morning, Ann has Ed buy several packages of thank you notes from the local card shop. She organizes herself outside under the apple trees in her chaise lounge, her table filled with cards and her notebook. "It's such a beautiful day, and we have to enjoy the day," she tells him as she organizes her little workstation. "Who knows when snow will come?"

"Well, that's hard to think about today. It's going to be very hot, so don't make plans to be out there the whole day."

"Just until lunchtime. Then I'll work in the house," Ann promises.

For the next week, Ann works like a woman on a mission. Every day, she works under the apple tree in the mornings, and when it gets too hot, she moves into the cool house. Ed watches as she works in her notebook and on her thank you cards. He knows she's intent on finishing her writing, but he's not sure he even wants to know what's consuming her.

On Friday at breakfast, Ann announces she's hoping to have her project finished later in the day. She has all her supplies in her arms as she starts to move outside to her place under the apple trees. "You know, you don't have to do it all in one week. You could spread it out," Ed comments, knowing full well that'll never happen.

"You're right, but once I get started, I hate to quit until the job's done. You understand, right?"

"Of course, sweetheart. Just let me know when they're ready to post, and I'll go up and get stamps. You do want me to mail them?" Ed inquires.

Although not many people actually use the post office these days, with e-mails and Internet and Facebook, Ann's old school upbringing and the fact that she actually enjoys doing her thank you cards the traditional way mean a trip to the post office once the cards are done.

"Do you mind?"

"No, not at all. Did I hear you tell Amy last night you're going to wear your monitor for the rest of the week?" Ed'd been so relieved when Amy told him last night.

"Well, if I put on the monitor, I don't have to go to her office so she can check me. It just makes better sense. We've got the technology; why not use it—unless you want to make a trip to the city." Ann already knows the answer to that.

"No, not if I don't have to. I think wearing the monitor is great. It makes me feel comfortable that I'm not going to find you in a heap somewhere in the house."

"Ed, you need to understand the monitor isn't going to keep me alive. I'm not going to live forever, and neither are you. It's not up to us to decide when we die; it's up to God. I have faith that God will let me come back to say good-bye to you. You have to have the same faith. Believe me, if I can find a way to send a message to you, I will. I need you to be sure you'll keep an open heart to get the message."

Ed grabs her and hugs her as hard as he can. "I love you so much." It's all Ed could get out before he breaks into sobs.

Ann drops her papers and returns the hug. They stand together for several minutes. The phone rings, but they leave it for voice mail until they hear Amy's cheerful voice. "Hi, Mom and Dad. Mom, just want to let you know the monitor's working and sending in a steady data stream. I'll call later. Love you both."

Ed lets Ann go and bends down to pick up her things. Ann quickly wipes away her tears. She smiles as he rises, and together they walk out to her little work area.

"Are you sure you don't mind me golfing with Al and the boys? I can always golf tomorrow if you'd rather I stick around and watch you write." Ed grins.

"No, I don't need a babysitter. You go have your round of golf. Call when you're done. Maybe the girls and I will meet you at the clubhouse for lunch."

Ed kisses her good-bye and heads off to pick up his clubs and go pick up Al. Al, as usual, will be waiting in the front of his house.

Ann sits back in her chaise. She has her pot of tea and her notepad. She needs to finish her letters to Ed, Amy, and Jake. She already has a list for Ed to work on. She knows he'll be relying on her to keep him moving, even after her death. She won't disappoint any of them, but she knows her time is very close. She has already labelled her jewellery and special things to make things easier for Ed.

Ann works steadily until she's finally finished. Feeling very complete, she lies back and gazes into the apple trees. The trees have always be a source of comfort for her. She remembers their first wedding anniversary, when her mom and dad dropped in with these two little trees. They resembled her broom handle, and they joked about how long it would take for the trees to produce apples. Today, their branches are bowing down, burdened with a bumper crop of delicious apples. Ed's been warning her for the past five years that the trees were getting old. Every year he cuts off the dead branches, and the following year there would be new growth. Ann read on the Internet that the trees could live for eighty years. And since they were only fifty years old, the trees have more life in them then either she or Ed.

She gazes over to the little marker they made when they buried Finnegan so long ago. He lived far longer than anyone expected, surpassing Dr. Dave's expectations. It was painful for Jake and Amy, especially Jake, when his best buddy was gone. At first, she thought a new puppy would work, but Jake was adamant: he didn't want a replacement for Finnegan. In his mind, there was no substitute for Finnegan. His love was for Finnegan, not some other dog. She eventually stopped asking if they wanted a dog. But now, perhaps a dog would be good for Ed. It would keep him active and give him someone else in the house. She picks up her lists and added a dog for Ed.

She lies back to listen to the neighbourhood noises and closes her eyes. She sees her parents and friends waiting at the gate. She knows it is her time. She knows she's finished what needed to be done here on earth and has faith that her family will manage without her earthly presence. Quietly and gracefully, she moves forward into the light and her new eternal life.

Her monitor sounds an alert to Amy. Amy's pager is in her locker. She's in the operating room at that moment, saving another life.

Chapter Thirty-Eight

It's a hot, sticky day, and the mood is sombre as Ann's friends and family gather in the cool basement of the church for lunch. Ann's celebration of life is exactly as she'd planned it, with her detailed instructions followed to the letter. The church is filled to capacity. In the early evening, the family would go to the cemetery for the casket's final destination. Ann made a very special list of her closest friends and family to be together to say their final good-bye.

Together, Jake and Amy deliver the eulogy. They each speak of their mother's love of life and her deep devotion to God and her family. They both recall that their mother had never raised her voice in anger in their entire lives. They spoke of the special memories and fun times together.

What they didn't speak about was their guilt at not being there for her in her last minutes. Ann had written to them about her peace at moving forward into her new eternal life and forbid them to feel remorse or guilt but to live their lives so she could be proud of them. These letters were private and neither Jake, Ed, nor Amy shared their personal letters. They held them close to their hearts with love and remembrance.

It's still hot and muggy as the small group of family and friends meet at the cemetery, next to the freshly dug hole. There is not a breeze to be had; the air is quiet, as if reflecting on the mood of those gathered.

Pastor James officiates. Pastor Ron is present in a wheelchair. He has come out of retirement to do one last favour for his dear friend. As Pastor Ron speaks, Ed feels a breeze against his ear, and in the distance, he hears Ann, "I love you. Keep strong and be there for Jake and Amy."

As tears roll down Amy's cheek, she also feels a breeze against her face and hears her mother's voice in her heart. "Amy, don't feel sorrow. Live your life and be happy. I love you."

Jake stands quietly as Pastor Ron quotes the scriptures. He has no more tears to shed; he was up all night, crying and remembering his mother. Finally, near dawn, he fell into a deep sleep and had a dream. He and his mother were walking along the beach as she talks to him. She tells him to be strong and watch out for his father and sister. She's left them each a list she expects them to complete. When Jake wakes, he feels an inner peace he's never felt before. He now knows he'll need to be there for his family, but he also knows they'll all be OK. His mother has prepared him to move forward, and he'll share this joy with his sister. He knows his father will join his mother when it's his time, but he believes that it will not be for some time yet.

Amy's surprised when she suddenly feels someone take hold of her hand. She looks up and stares into the eyes of Christopher Laing. She has not seen him in such a long time. Amy can't believe he came. They had been friends since the Booster Mind Team days. She visited him when he was at Yale with Jake. It was during that first visit that Amy decided she wanted to go to Yale, too. They spent time together while she was there. After she left Yale, Christopher and Jake kept in communication, and after graduation, they became partners in the same law firm in Toronto. She hasn't seen him since their evening together at Jake's farewell party. They might have had a future together if they both hadn't been so driven to succeed down their respective career choices.

Next to him, stands his sister, Victoria. Amy's even more surprised. They must have come out together. Victoria's taken hold of Jake's arm.

No one wants to leave the cemetery, but finally, as dusk settles, the small group reluctantly breaks up and everyone heads to their vehicle in their own individual silence. Jake puts his arms around his sister and his father as they walk back to his car. "We have a lot to do to get everything on Mom's list done. I promised her I'd start my list in the morning."

Christopher and Victoria move forward to stand by Jake's car, leaving their friends to say their final good-byes alone. They stand, watching and waiting for their long time friends.

"Thank you for coming." Jake hugs Christopher. "Did you fly in today from Toronto?"

"Sure did. I wanted to be with my best friends in their time of sorrow. Your mom was always so kind to both Victoria and I while we were at school in Huntersville. Boarding at the college wasn't the greatest thing, and you guys are like family to us. Of course we'd come."

"We're going back to the house. Do you want to join us?" Amy softly inquires.

Victoria looks over at Ed, "Perhaps it would be easier if we go out for dinner and not bother your dad at the house. He's probably had so much company; he might want to be alone for a while."

"No. I don't want to go out for dinner with anyone. I want to go back to the house with Dad." Everyone looks shocked at Amy's tone and conviction.

Ed knows what he has to tell Amy's going to be hard, but she's in the most pain and needs to see life goes on, and she has to go on as well. "Actually, if you don't mind, I want to be alone tonight. I haven't been able to bear the thought of opening the envelope your mother left me, but now I feel I'm ready. I hope you don't mind."

"No, Dad. I understand you need your time. I'll join Jake for dinner. Otherwise, he'll pester me forever. But, for the record, I'm not going to enjoy myself." Amy has no more tears left to cry. She just has a dull, sad headache that goes all the way down to her heart.

"In that case, let's meet back at the house. We can drop off Dad and let him have some quiet time." Jake opens the door for Ed to get into the car.

Together, they drive up to the house and arrive at the same time Christopher drives up. His sister hops out of the car and embraces Jake. "Sorry I didn't get a chance to speak with you earlier. Your mom was one special lady. I've never seen a place as packed in my life. Gives me an idea of what a sardine feels like." Victoria's just as flamboyant as Amy remembers, and she can't help but notice how Jake's face comes alive when Victoria's around.

Christopher moves toward Amy and hugs her. "It's been a long time, Amy. You look as stunning as the last time I saw you, at Jake's Toronto office farewell party."

He reaches across Amy and shakes Ed's hand. "It's been a long time, sir. Do you remember me?"

Ed remembers. "Of course I do. You and your sister were members of the Booster Mind Team. You like ketchup on your green beans."

They all laugh. "He actually hates ketchup now," Victoria teases. "I'm sure Heinz stocks took a nosedive when he decided to go cold turkey."

"I discovered salt instead," Christopher replies. "Jake, you must be starving. It's been," Christopher checks his watch with great flourish, "at least three hours since your last snack."

"It's good to know some things never change." Victoria takes Amy's hand. "Do you need to freshen up?"

Ann glances at her father. She understands what he needs to do, and she knows what she must do as well. "No, I think I'm fine—unless you think I should maybe reapply some makeup."

"You're great just the way you are." Victoria gives Amy a quick hug. "You've always looked beautiful with your gorgeous hair and great completion. Do you know how envious I've always been?

With that, Amy moves toward her father. She gives him a hug and kiss. "I'll call you later tonight. I love you, Dad."

Christopher grabs her hand and escorts her off to his car. "Jake, you and Victoria can follow in your car. Meet you in Airdrie at Paul's Steak House."

Before Amy can protest, the car door is opened. Christopher helps her into the car.

Ed waves as both cars drive away. He sees his friends and neighbours, standing outside watching. They'll be his lifelines and support as he moves forward. He smiles and waves at them as well. They return his wave and watch as he turns to go inside. They're close friends and will be there for him. Besides, Ann left them each an envelope and list as well. With a heavy heart, Ed goes into the house, knowing he'll move forward. But, he also believes it's going to be a difficult and lonely road in spite of his friends and family.

Ann did get her wish for one last chance to spend a few minutes with her family. She knows her prayers have been answered, and she's seen the future and the happiness her family will share. There will be marriages and babies. While there'll be bumps in the road, she knows that love will keep her family together. Ann also knows she won't be together with Ed for a while. It's not his time.

Acknowledgements

I want to thank my daughter for her love and belief in me. The tears she shed while she read my notes and completed chapters persuaded me to believe this book was worthy of completion and publication. Thanks to my daughter-in-law who kept me going, as she daily checked to see how much I had accomplished the previous night. Once she read the book, she motivated me into thinking about developing and giving each of the characters their own stories. Special thanks go to my son for his knowledge and strength. He provided me with firsthand details of tornados based on his own experience. While he was on the road, my daughter-in-law would read sections for his comment and input. I am grateful to my grandson, Kolby, for his words of advice from his teenage prospective, many of his suggestions are incorporated. This support encouraged me to continue. I also want to acknowledge my grandsons, sisters, nieces, and nephews, who have all been a great inspiration to me. I hope you can see yourselves in my writing. I love you all very much.

A special thanks goes to the wonderful women and men at FriesenPress for all their support and assistance in taking my document and converting it into a published book.

I hope you will look for more of my books to discover what happens to Amy, Jake, and the rest of their families.

Coming soon...

In the next book, you can read about Amy's story and her efforts to find the love and the companionship her parents had. Amy has a struggle, since she must learn how to give up her workaholic ways and juggle a career and a life. By working through the list her mother left her, Amy begins to find the joy in life and slowly starts to find peace and contentment for herself. Fortunately, she learns to find time for her friends and learns about love. Does she succeed, or will her career continue to get in the way of her happiness? Ann knew her family would be fine and had faith that by using the list she left each one, her family could find happiness.

I want to share the recipe for Ann's favourite dessert, Pecan Ganache, since it's one of my favourite desserts. It's so easy and quick to make. It can be made a day or two ahead of time, and you can garnish it on the plate with all sorts of fun. A sprinkle of cocoa powder, a swirl of chocolate, a drizzle of caramel ice cream topping: let your imagination be your guide. Everyone I serve wants the recipe. I hope you enjoy it as much as I do.

Ann's Favourite Pecan Ganache

1 cup light Karo corn syrup

3 eggs, slightly beaten

2/3 cups granulated sugar

3 tbsp butter, melted

2 tsp pure vanilla extract

2 cups whole pecans

1 unbaked pie crust. You can use homemade or store bought

Heat the oven to 350°F. In a large bowl, add the first 5 ingredients. Mix well. Line the piecrust with the pecans, gently pushing them into the pastry. Pour in the ingredients. Bake 50–60 minutes. You will know when it is done when you insert a knife into the center of the pie and it comes out clean. Let the pie cool slightly. While it is cooling, make the chocolate ganache.

2/3 cup whipping cream

2 tbsp butter

6 oz dark chocolate, either chips or cut into chunks

(You can use semi-sweet or milk, depending on your tastes. My favourite is dark.)

Heat the cream and butter, DO NOT LET IT BOIL. Once it is hot, remove from the burner and stir in the chocolate.

As soon as the chocolate is completely melted, pour over the warm pie. Let it cool until the bottom of the pan is just warm to the touch and then refrigerate. It can be stored for two days, not that it will last that long.

Have fun using this ganache part of the recipe; it works great on all sorts of pastries and desserts.

CPSIA information can be obtained at www.ICGtesting.com
Printed in the USA
LVOW08s1537230813

349024LV00001BB/18/P

9 781460 215951